Double Happiness

Also by Mary-Beth Hughes

Wavemaker II

MARY-BETH HUGHES

Double Happiness

Stories

Black Cat
New York
a paperback original imprint of Grove/Atlantic, Inc.

These stories first appeared in the following publications:
"Pelican Song" in *The Paris Review*
"Horse"in *The Saint Ann's Review*
"Blue Grass" in *The Georgia Review*
"Rome" in *The Mississippi Review*
"Israel" in *Ploughshares*
"Double Happiness," "The Widow of Combarelles,"
and "May Day" in *A Public Space*

Printed in the United States of America

FIRST EDITION

ISBN: 978-0-8021-7074-3

Black Cat
a paperback original imprint of Grove/Atlantic Inc.
841 Broadway
New York, NY 10003

Distributed by Publishers Group West

www.groveatlantic.com

10 11 12 13   10 9 8 7 6 5 4 3 2 1

For Claire,
and for Timmy,
with love.

Contents

Double Happiness

Pelican Song

I WAS THE KIND OF THIRTY-YEAR-OLD WHO HAD ONLY recently left adolescence behind. I was mostly a modern dancer. I rehearsed, I went to class. I worked the concession stand in an art-movie theater where actors and filmmakers ushered. A novelist with strong powers of concentration manned the ticket booth. I had a studio apartment in Gramercy Park that looked out on an ivied brick wall. When I wanted to get out of the city I would take the bus to visit my mother in central Jersey. My mother was far along into her second marriage. She and her husband had built a house in an abandoned peach orchard with the proceeds from the sale of my childhood home and his antique-car-supply boutique. They acted as their own general contractors and saved a lot of money. Now that the house was finished they had their collective eye open for an investment scheme.

Like the ticket taker, the man my mother married was really a novelist. My mother created an author's den for him in the upper portion of their beautiful new house. She decorated it with my lost father's old desk, very attractive and manly with brass inlays, and his leather chair. Everything faced out over the inground swimming pool and the putting green, and beyond that to the old orchard and then the woods. Couldn't be more inspiring, everyone said.

My mother, always interested in words, took seriously, in a way lost to the world with my generation, the role of helpmate. She typed her husband's manuscripts, judiciously editing them as she went along. She served lunch on a tray, left atop a small marble pedestal outside the den door. And she checked the mailbox at the end of the long drive for the latest news from his literary agent. If there was another rejection waiting, she prepared the gentlest delivery.

At the art-movie theater in the West Village we took failure for granted. In the house in the orchard the stakes were much higher. Each time a rejection letter came, though often flattering, even encouraging, it represented an enormous blow to the whole enterprise. Even so, I decided to try my own hand at fiction writing. I joined a group. I wrote one-paragraph stories that I liked to read out loud to my mother over her kitchen speakerphone while she was preparing the meals that went upstairs. For Christmas that year, my mother's husband gave me a lovely, quite serious pen, with a kind note folded inside the box. But at the movie theater no one allowed my ministories any more importance than my modern dance performances. My biggest obstacle to respect, however, had to do with men.

I had an odd figure for a modern dancer. Rubenesque, my composer boyfriend called my body when pressed for compliments. This was long before I found the tiny crimson panties tucked beneath his buckwheat pillow. I also heard him say Rembrandt. My mother, it's worth noting, took figures very seriously. I often felt this was another feature of her generation, like the typing and the meals on trays. In my time, I believed, a body could be different and still be okay. But when the composer mentioned Botero, I lost confidence.

After the panty disclosure, I started seeing a painting student. He ushered part-time and still lived with his parents on the Upper East Side. His beard had developed only under his mouth and nose so far, and though born at New York Hospital he spoke with an English accent. Some days I'd meet him after class at Cooper Union. He was a freshman. I felt like his nanny waiting at the curb. But he was understanding, in a way I think was more intense because he was still living at home, when I began getting the late-night phone calls from my mother.

The calls started some time after the Christmas I received the pen. I'd come by myself for the holiday; the painter had his own plans with his mother and father. I stayed Christmas night in the guest suite next to the writing den. My presents made a nice pile at the foot of the bed, and I must have slept late, because when I got up the sun was high over the snow-covered putting green and I could smell coffee long past its first perc wafting from the room next door. My mother's husband tended to stay all day in the writing den so I didn't change out of my pajamas, just went downstairs to find my mother and scare up some breakfast.

At the foot of the stairs I heard a loud bang. My mother was a big redecorator, so I assumed she was moving a sofa, and then I heard a louder bang, more like a chest of drawers against a wall. Voices like growls could only be the television tuned to a low volume, so as not to disturb the writing process.

I took a quick look at the manger display my mother had set out in the foyer—sweet, a big part of my childhood. Even the hay was arranged nicely and all the ceramic farm animals had pleasant shapes. I heard the word *cunt* quite distinctly from the kitchen and turned my head. The chest of drawers banged against a wall one more time. My mother had painted an old heavy cabinet with white enamel, and I thought—without really thinking—she might be wrestling it into place.

But then I felt a strange fear that buckled my legs as I rounded the corner into the kitchen and found my mother backed against the wall, her husband pressed up hard against her, his face purple. I wasn't sure what I was seeing, and when they both turned to look at me, my mother laughed but with an odd kind of disdain. She pushed her husband off her. He said something about coffee and left the room through the dining-room door.

I didn't know what to ask, and my head hurt as if it were my skull that had been bounced. My mother attended to her hair. She coughed and smiled. Lifted a hand and her eyebrows as if to curtail the next obvious thing I might say, and walked past me through the door I'd entered to meet her husband at the manger. But he'd beaten her to the foyer and was already upstairs, walking slowly—I could hear him above me—down the long book-lined hallway to the writing den.

My mother's husband didn't just want to write novels, he wanted to write best sellers. At the art-movie theater we understood what he would never believe, which was that no one— we liked to talk in terms of multiple lightning strikes; we weren't entirely original in this—got the recognition they deserved. We tended to read, perform, and scrutinize, often with devastating candor, each other's work. We were envious, back-biting, and deeply critical, even scathing and destructive during lag-time discussions in our polyester smocks. We were lucky though. We had a context, and we had an audience, and there were more than two of us. When things got too painful we switched our shifts. My mother and her husband only had each other, in a house that they'd built to be so graceful and accommodating they'd never have to leave it.

When my mother called me on Valentine's Day eve from the local Hilton, which she said was perfectly charming, two towns away from their home, I was surprised, but not entirely. She just wanted me to know where she was in case I needed her. She was fine. Her husband was working very hard and wanted a little privacy. Did I think cranberry velvet seat cushions would be pretty in the dining room? I had no opinion on this, and wrote down her room number at the Hilton. The next afternoon she called to say she was home and sending me something special. A beautiful dictionary arrived in a day or so inscribed with love from the two of them.

I was a little worried about my mother, but I had romantic problems of my own. I may have underestimated the maturity level of the painting student because he was such a fine kisser, and his drawings were intricate and intelligent. For Valentine's Day he wrote my name in pink rose petals on the covered stoop of my apartment building and then lay down naked there in the cold, but not snowy, night, and waited for me to come home from the art-movie theater. He was very slender, and the chill he caught kept him out of classes for two full months. His parents didn't appreciate my sickroom visits. The housekeeper looked genuinely alarmed to see a robust thirty-year-old teetering at the end of his trundle bed, so we communicated by late-night phone calls, which his mother listened to, breathing with complete audibility, on the extension. He couldn't wait until he'd gotten through art school so that he could just make his own money and leave. It was oppressive and he had the courage to say so.

My painter friend was still malingering when my mother's husband's father died. An old bear, someone who felt cruelly was power. And in a way it was. No holiday was ever complete until old Sven had dialed in to ridicule the hopes of his aging son. Novelist-smovelist, his voice boomed through the kitchen over the speakerphone like he was actually making sense.

Just unplug the bastard, I suggested. And though my mother cast a weary eye when I said such things, her husband ignored me. He did this in a noble way that suggested strong men listen to the ravings of their fathers.

But it turned out I was a prophet. Old Sven's brain blew a gasket early in the new year. My mother's husband, who had power of attorney, pulled the plug in record time. And so, during the first big holiday gathering without Sven, the Easter egg hunt, there was a peculiar silence. And everyone, I could sense, believed this was somehow my fault.

My mother called me after that to change our Mother's Day plans. Why didn't I come to the Hilton? she said. There was a great indoor pool, and a sauna. I could share her suite and we could have a really good time. Because it was an unusually mild spring in the West Village, I was able to get the weekend off. Who wanted to go to the movies when cherry blossoms were sprinkling café tables?

I took the bus to Freehold. My mother was waiting in her little blue sport Caddy, wearing wraparound sunglasses from the seventies. Traditionally she liked to leap out of the car and hug me like I'd just finished my first full day at preschool, but today, and maybe she was anxious to show me the pool, she just started the engine and waved her left hand. I dipped down into the passenger bucket and took a good look before speaking. It wasn't just the sling, it was the way she didn't seem able to turn her head. And when she lifted her free hand to the wheel it was swollen like a mitt, her knuckles strafed with red slashes.

Even facing straight ahead she could still issue the look not to say anything. You want to wait until we're at the Hilton? I said. She laughed. We weren't going to the Hilton, it turned out. We were staying with a friend, Faye, who had lent my mother, for the purpose of this holiday visit, the guest cottage on her waterfront property. You'll love this, she said, you've always loved the water. I couldn't remember loving the water, but was sure my mother was right.

Faye had problems of her own. Her thieving ex-husband had run off with the golf club locker-room attendant she'd over-tipped for years. It was disgusting! Even so, Faye had taken time to fill the larder and the bar at the guest cottage, and she let it be known, before going off to the lawyer to skewer her lousy ex, that if my mother's husband put one foot on her property he'd regret it. My mother sighed, and smiled her gratitude. But when the sound of Faye's MG died out, my mother explained that Faye was consumed by rage. It was a terrible, wasteful shame.

Faye's cottage had twin chaises that looked out from the veranda to the bay. In the early evening light, sailboats bumped and tilted around delicate crescent waves. The sun went down, turning everything pink for a while, and my mother's face behind her sunglasses looked a little less distorted. She told me there'd been a particularly harsh rejection letter that week, and now the novel was dead. Which novel? I asked. I knew there had been several. My mother was quiet. A small boat tacked back straight into the last sliver of sun. Mom?

Maybe all of them. It's possible.

I was quiet, out of respect, but then said, Sometimes people just feel that way. I told her the story of despair and renewal at the movie theater. An actor-usher who'd met Francis Ford Coppola at the McDonald's on Sixth Avenue was now a night intern at his literary magazine. Who knows what will happen next? And he'd just about given up! And what about my own friend whose oppressive home environment and fevers cut his art down to bare scratches for a while? Second runner-up in the Cooper Union Gesture Drawing Competition last Monday! And what about me?

Sweetheart, you're a dreamer. She gave me a one-cornered close-mouthed smile that was a dead ringer for her husband's. I'd seen this smile before, trotted out for this very subject. Her husband was a professional. It was different. They weren't children.

Well, I'm not exactly a child, either, I said. But I was, her nonreply said. And this came down to the checks she sent me, and the cash gifts, and the winter coats and boots I got for nearly every birthday, and the microwave and the matched living-room set. And the arrangement she'd made years ago with my co-op board and with Con Ed. I paid for my own transportation and food out of the paycheck from the art-movie theater, but the rest, as everyone who came to my mother's house knew, and about which old Sven had been particularly vocal, basically came from my allowance. Meanwhile, my mother's smug friends' children were busy working out plans for third babies and second homes. Even Faye had a daughter with a time-share in Aspen.

The financial side of pursuing our art wasn't subject to the deep truth-telling we otherwise advocated at the movie theater. I liked to quote Virginia Woolf to myself, now that I was leaning toward fiction, about the five-hundred pounds and the lonely room. Was there some caveat about not getting that from your mother?

My mother gently pressed her vodka collins up against her face and squinted at the dark water. The reflection of the tiki torches looked like jellyfish wriggling on the black surface.

Maybe you'd like to hear my new story?

Darling, you'll wreck your eyes reading in the dark.

It's short, I'll recite it!

Oh, bunny. Well.

But then the gunshot revs of Faye's MG sounded in the gravel beside the guest cottage. Did I imagine my mother's relief? There, suddenly, was Faye, hopping mad, sucker punching the hydrangea. The scum had married the locker-room floozy.

Could we believe it? My mother was lovely and magnanimous. Something like this, she knew, could never happen to her. She said sweet, smart things that made Faye laugh.

I was still thinking about my story, maybe Faye would like to hear it? My mother offered to mix some healing martinis. But Faye said she'd do it herself. With that hand—she tipped her perky head at my mother's sling—they'd be slugging down pure vermouth. At this, Faye and my mother made little mews with their mouths at the same time, and I was startled that my mother could be so friendly, so intimate, with a female who wasn't me. This seemed new.

But the biggest news, along with the disastrous rejection letter, was that old Sven had done something naughty with his will. Faye and my mother hunkered down, stem glasses balanced in the air, to talk it over. It turned out he'd left an enormous chunk to the Author's Guild! And on a cruel Post-it, in a scrawly hand, he'd written to my mother's husband: For your colleagues, thought you'd be pleased.

He wasn't, my mother said, and Faye slid her an appreciative glance. Both drained their glasses, and I offered again to recite my story. Sweetness, they drawled out in tandem, then collapsed into giggles. Unstoppable giggles, they bent their sculptural coifs over slim, extended legs and roared. Oh god. Darling, my mother tried, and then waved her swollen hand quickly as if shooing a mosquito, and Faye laughed harder still. Finally, Faye stood and coughed to say she'd handle this. Though her eyes were still weeping with laughter, her mouth looked somber. My angel, she addressed me, and my mother kept her face tilted down. Don't you think your mother has had just about enough literature for today? I'd say, really, enough for a lifetime? Yes?

Oh, Faye, stop, my mother said. Sweetie, I'll hear your story in the car tomorrow, um? Faye, stop it. Then I can really concentrate. Okay?

That's okay.

Good girl, said Faye.

Sweetheart, my mother sighed.

Don't worry about it.

Well, maybe when it's a little longer than a paragraph you'll send it to me and I can take a good hard look.

It's supposed to be a paragraph.

Faye smirked, and now that it was really dark outside, my mother took off her sunglasses and gave her a serious look. But that communication was lost because my mother's eyes were so swollen, so deeply purpled and bruised even in the dim light of the tiki torches, that Faye stopped laughing and put down her stem glass.

I'm calling Lou, said Faye. Lou was her scum of an ex-husband. But he was also an orthopedic surgeon. My mother said, Absolutely not. But Faye plugged her ears with soft-looking fingers and marched straight into the guesthouse. Lou arrived within fifteen minutes. He and Faye were surprisingly cordial for two people who hated each other's guts. Lou remembered me fondly from golf-club brunches when I was a child and then forgot me completely while he dressed my mother's wounds in the surgical light of Faye's guest dressing room. He gave my mother a sedative. In the morning she was very tired, so Faye drove me to the bus.

I had to work that afternoon at the movie theater and my mother had urged me to go. Don't worry, my mother said. She was incredibly sleepy. Don't worry, Faye said. Don't worry, said the painter when I told him on the phone.

Soon after that, my legs began to give out spontaneously; I didn't even have to think about my mother. My legs would wobble out of the blue and then hip, knee, ankle would collapse in a ripple. It made it tricky to walk. The steps down to the subway, which I was obliged to take from Gramercy Park to the movie theater, became a challenge. This wouldn't have been that big a deal, since I was already making the transition from modern dance to fiction writing, but I did have one last performance scheduled at the famous White Columns. My "Pelican Song," old Sven had called it over the speakerphone at Christmas. His last pronouncement, as it turned out. My mother and her husband had always planned to attend. They'd sent a giant check to the choreographer during his holiday fundraiser. And he'd tacked on a three-minute solo at the end of the piece, "Wings of Love," for me. Now the performance was minutes away. And my sudden leg-melts were trying the patience of even this well-funded choreographer.

I decided to address my condition by writing about it. Master the problem by making it conscious. So I began work on a full-scale paragraph to describe what I understood about my mother and her husband. This was more difficult than I'd guessed. In my mother's husband's novels, the women, I knew from several brief glances over the years, had fabulous, surprisingly active nipples, and insatiable appetites for very straight-ahead penis-worshipping sex acts. In my paragraph, there was sex, certainly, but of a different order.

The two weeks between my Mother's Day visit and the performance were terrible. The worry, the rehearsals, the distress of composition (I began, oddly, to sympathize about this with my mother's husband). And the rain. Every single day. I was forced to work double shifts pouring bagged popcorn into the pretend popper unit. Everyone in the West Village was coming to the movies, it seemed. By the time I got home each night, it was late, and the phone at Faye's guest cottage rang and rang.

My painter finally recovered enough to spend a night of love on my air mattress. We jiggled and drooled and painted our chests with Nutella. When the phone blared after midnight we assumed it was his mother, who'd insisted on taking my number. But the answering machine speaker played out an echoing voice in the little room that, even without words, only crying, I knew was my own mother instead. I scrambled to pluck up the receiver. Wait, wait, I said. Hello?

She was still there, breathing hard, whimpering, Darling? And now I felt my sternum shudder and give. Where are you? I asked.

At home. She was locked in her bathroom, the one with the pinwheel wallpaper, the Jacuzzi tub, and the pocket door she had long debated: solid core or green glass? I could hear, even behind her harsh breathing, the bang of a fist against the swirly maple she'd finally picked and a muffled growl just like old Sven warming up for his holiday message. It's locked, she said. I listened. The window, she said. And I thought hard. The window opened onto a trellis that reached down to a patio which bounded the putting green. If she pushed her pelvis— she didn't like that word; hips then, I said, keep your hips close to the wall of the house. She could probably shimmy down.

That's crazy, said the painter, and laughed. (That laugh ended our relationship.) Flush the toilet, I said in a whisper, as if her husband could hear me, flush before you open the latch. I would get the next bus to Freehold. Just walk into town, can you do that?

Of course, she said, putting me in my place. If she could get out the window, she'd see me there. He called me a sick, rotting cunt? she said, as a question, as if reviewing whether she was making the right move.

Well, you're not, I said. Be careful of your feet. There might be broken glass.

Sweetheart, she whispered, for goodness sake.

My mother was a woman who dressed for bed. When the bus pulled in at the all-night diner in Freehold I scanned beyond the parking lot for where her cream satin peignoir might be flitting through the holly bushes. The exhaust-smelling heat of the bus had made the Nutella gluey. My sleep T-shirt stuck to my chest. I backed down the exit steps, uncertain. The bus driver stared at me. Eyes on the road, you pervert, I barked, then felt ashamed. My mother would be ashamed, too, if she'd heard me.

I had a coat for her and some shoes. Sneakers are for athletes, she always maintained. So I carried my only pair of black slingbacks and a lovely silk overcoat she'd given me, but no money. I'd borrowed the fare from the painter. Now, I realized, as the bus chugged away and the quiet settled in, that my mother probably didn't have much cash on her, either. Didn't matter. First I'd find her, and then, once she was appropriately dressed, we'd hitchhike our way to Faye's guest cottage.

Was it an hour? It's hard to know in the dark. But eventually, when she didn't show up, I began the long walk past the cornfields to her house. I was shivering though the weather was balmy, and I was hungry. Each lumpy-looking shadow made me afraid I might find her lying by the side of the road like some fallen animal. But I didn't find her. When I came to the end of her drive the house was lit as if for a holiday party. The button lights glowed to trace the curve of the the drive through the fragrant peach trees. The deep porch, its long planters thick with ivy and juniper, was aglow. It seemed every room was lit: the writer's den, the guest suite, all the reception rooms, the master bedroom. Around back the garage doors were flung open as if the party might flood into its bays. The blue Caddy my mother liked to drive was parked close to the mudroom door, but the Mercedes, her husband's staid sedan, was missing. I didn't need to go inside the house to know she wasn't there.

My dearest heart, my mother wrote to me. *You'll find it strange, I know, but we've flown away to try again. It's difficult for a writer, maybe for any true artist, to make a good life here. Old Sven was kinder to you than to his own son, as you will see from the enclosed. I love you more than anything, always have, always will.*

My birth date was penciled on the envelope. A bonded courier slid it beneath my door. The letter was typed and unsigned. The bank check was for a hundred-thousand dollars.

The house in the orchard was sold by old Sven's personal lawyer in a private auction. He phoned me about furniture and, of course, the manger, but I didn't want anything. This lawyer tells me from time to time, when I press, that they are both fine, they are in a quiet place now, they just need a little peace. He tells me that my mother sends her best love, as though she's right there waiting on another extension. Sometimes I think my mother is still looking for me. She just doesn't recognize me in my suit and leather shoes. Sometimes I scan the back pages of books. I pay close attention to long murder mysteries with women as dispensable, secondary characters. I read the acknowledgments, especially of the authors with phony-sounding names, hoping he will have the courage someday to say how amazing she was, how beautiful, and how she made everything, absolutely everything, possible.

Horse

WHEN ISABEL STEPPED FROM HER HONEYMOON BED AND drew the drapes, the view of Atlantic City was awful. Tilted houses, scattered parking lots, municipal buildings rusty from the sea air. The arrangement seemed badly planned or not planned at all, and the elevation of their bedroom was wasted because the ocean was out of sight. Just behind me, Isabel thought. She turned as if to find it there. Tom was sleeping. His lips sometimes vibrated on the exhale. I have wasted him with kisses, she thought. Or at least she hoped she had. Marriage required a certain alignment of mind and body, and she was determined to make good on her end.

Isabel left the window and went in to draw her first bath in the heart-shaped tub. She chose the lavender bubble bath. She tried to remember, lavender was for fidelity? Lavender was for kindness? She couldn't recall but earnestly allowed its stream to join the bath water. She was twenty-two. The year was 1967.

At noon, a tiny bellboy, probably not more than fourteen years old, wheeled in breakfast. As the boy backed out the door, Tom, who was barely sitting up, reached for various pockets, but couldn't find anything smaller than a twenty and said he would catch him later. The bellboy nodded and smiled, but when Tom rose from the blankets and went into the bathroom, Isabel retrieved a five-dollar bill from her purse and settled the account on the spot. The moment the door whispered shut, she felt uneasy, almost dizzy, and hoped Tom would forget all about the bellboy. She imagined Tom's confusion when the boy said he'd been tipped, overtipped. Already she was making mistakes. She fiddled with the silvery tops on the dishes, piling them into an awkward stack before Tom came to the table. He mentioned his eggs were cold.

Breakfast was brief. They were both anxious to get on with the day. Tom hurried into his clothes, barely glancing at Isabel as she sat legs crossed in her new stockings, new shoes, pretty new dress. It was only in the lobby, heading across the massive expanse of green carpet, that Tom pulled her to him. She was walking slightly ahead, looking in her purse for a booklet on sights she had borrowed. He pulled her to him, as if overwhelmed by the sight of her, and kissed her just beneath the earlobe, and whispered, My sweet wife. She felt her heart would break open with relief. She was certain she heard the word *newlyweds* whispered by admiring bystanders she sensed all about them. The word danced very lightly on the air: *newlyweds*.

Beyond the gilded doors she could see how thick and gray the day had become. The cold was nearly visible. She pulled her collar high on her pearl-colored coat, winter-white, a bridal coat, and snuggled against Tom's arm. The boardwalk was immensely broad, its slats of wood arranged like a herringbone fabric. The waves sputtered and coughed a gray spume far to the left. So far away they seemed like a reel of film draped across the low horizon. Isabel nonetheless was transfixed by the sight of the drab sea. She'd grown up inland and was unaccustomed to water sprawling just out of reach.

Tom released his arm from Isabel's and scratched his bare head. Sweetheart, you forgot your hat! Isabel almost said, then stopped. She satisfied the impulse with a brief loving stroke across his windblown hair, then devoted herself to the pages of her tour book and was pleased to find something that would interest them both. The World Famous Diving Horse! Certainly better than skeet ball or the merry-go-round. It wasn't far, according to the map, and open year-round. So much was still closed in March.

Tom was willing to be led to the exhibition pier until a better idea presented itself. Did Isabel want to get a drink? Why not? They were on vacation. Honeymoon! Isabel cried. But she wanted to see the horse, didn't Tom? They could go watch, it wouldn't take long, and then they could go have a drink.

It was farther than Isabel's map had indicated. By the time they reached the pier, Isabel's cheeks were chafed from the cold.

Tom's gloved hands were deep in his pockets, his collar pulled nearly over his ears. They paid the three-dollar admission then went inside through a low damp tunnel that led to the end of the pier. They were well out into the ocean when they emerged to find a rather rickety arrangement, something like a small arena. Not very sturdy, Isabel thought. The planks rigged for seating looked barely stable. One whole side of the tiny stadium was completely open and a large chunk of gray ocean was revealed in the breach. The sky looked like the water, just a white shade of gray with brackish clouds bumping against each other. A harsh wind scorched through the opening. Tom and Isabel waited perhaps ten minutes for the other spectators to arrive, but no one else came.

Finally, a gate was released on a platform high above them. The platform had a long tongue, which extended through the gap and over a patch of ocean. Three men struggled above to bring a white horse, a beautiful, mammoth white horse, out onto the stand. Its eyes were covered with blinders, but even so it seemed to sense the waves were sharp and unwelcoming. Isabel thought its eyes must be very gentle, very kind. Some animals had very knowing eyes. She could tell, even from a distance, the white horse was one of them. The men struggled to get the horse to move forward, but it wouldn't, and each progression toward the sea was accomplished by the horse being dragged as though its hooves were skates across the wood planking, and each forward pull was followed by a desperate skittering back.

Stupid horse, Tom said. What? said Isabel. But Tom didn't even look at her. He had his wallet out and was counting the bills inside. I'm not staying for this, he said, it's a waste of time and money, and he stood up, indicating that they should leave. Well, said Isabel, stalling until she had a clear idea of what to say. She looked up at the horse. It was on its hind legs, its hooves drawn close to its heart. How could she leave? I think we should stay, she said to Tom, I think the horse will jump, don't you? Fine, he said, stay, and before she knew it he was ducking into the tunnel.

It had happened so suddenly. They had had a fight, or it seemed as if they had and Isabel didn't know why. She sat, too confused to follow him and ask what was wrong. She huddled in her coat, which was far too thin for the gusts blowing off the water, and felt a sticky darkness opening up inside of her. She sat there, unable to budge, and watched the horse being coaxed into a dive. Now the men had something tempting in their hands. They waved some treat over the edge of the platform so the horse would be fooled into jumping, but still the horse stayed, impervious to threat or seduction. Isabel couldn't stop watching. When the horse went up on its hind legs she felt she understood that better than anything she'd ever known. She understood that drawing in, the way the horse's head lifted back and to the side, away from the foolish men. She understood all that.

Someone was gently touching her shoulder. She turned, so relieved. Of course he'd come back. She knew he would, even if she'd been afraid to think it. But it was the attendant from the admission gate offering Isabel her money back. Isabel shook her head, no, it was all right, she didn't want her money. The horse had done the right thing, she said, made the right decision, it's too cold to jump into the ocean today.

When the horse was finally led off the platform and the gate had been bolted, Isabel stood, wrapped her coat tighter around her body, and prepared to return to the hotel.

When she unlocked the door of their suite, Tom's back was to her. He sat slumped in the black-leather armchair, facing the television. Someone had sent flowers. Plump irises sheathed in pink cellophane were uncentered on the coffee table, the card still sealed. Tom was having his drink. He set a miniature empty bottle down by way of greeting. She approached him unsure what to say. He didn't ask her anything, didn't say hello. His face didn't have that hinged-shut look he had when he was angry. Still, there was nothing to guide her, nothing to signal her.

She opened the drapes wider. He didn't stop her or comment. He watched the television screen with indifference. Isabel shook back the gauzy sheers in the windows so the whole of the sky and the topsy-turvy buildings were laid out in their unpredictable pattern before her. She pulled her coat close to her chest though the steam heat was stifling, and turned to watch her husband. After a very long while, when he didn't say anything, she told him, deliberately, on that first full day of their marriage, that the horse had jumped. The horse jumped, she said. It was incredible, she said. Then she stepped up onto their double honeymoon bed without removing her coat or shoes. She let the black heels scar the silver spread. She didn't care. She lifted her legs up and down, shoes scraping against the bedspread, and held her arms tucked in close to her, bare hands balled like hooves. She couldn't help it. She twisted her head back and let out a cry. The horse jumped she said, and Tom got up from his chair, a little afraid. My God, Isabel, he said, and thought she was the prettiest thing he'd ever seen. She teetered on the edge of the bed, her arms starting to wilt, her face wrecked for a cry.

Come on, Isabel, he whispered, opening his arms. He gently pushed the black chair out of the way. Come on, Isabel, he said and bit down on his lip when he stepped forward needing to catch her.

Blue Grass

WHEN I SEE A PRETTY WOMAN NOW, I NO LONGER SAY to myself, Nice face. Instead, I think, There's someone Sonny could love. If I'm sitting in a coffee shop, I sink behind my cup and hand him over. I imagine him looking at her obliquely, then full on, then straight into her eyes because some tilt of a lash tells him her beauty runs deep.

Lately I find myself making pilgrimages to Saks Fifth Avenue. I listen to the saleswoman talk about anything, even how everyone paid cash this Christmas, so that she will tell me what I really want to know: some device or potion, some answer. The person I talk to most is Rita. She doesn't wear a tag, only a discreet SFA enameled clip attached to a cunningly draped scarf. I know her name because of the embarrassing number of visits I've paid to her counter.

Rita has several bottles of lotion arrayed on the glass top. She slips a hand across the lids like a conjurer who will sense the vibration of the most appropriate liquid. Her hand pauses above a squat bottle of vivid yellow gel, which she then slides forward. I pick it up, bring it close to my face, but the color makes me skeptical enough to replace it on the glass without opening it. Rita's lips barely purse. She leans down, keeping her head above the counter like a swimmer, and retrieves a smaller brown vial from below. I examine her skin as I always do when I see her, scanning for improvements that are never as dramatic as I would hope, and this disappointment deploys a childhood memory:

I was at the pharmacy where the word *Beauty* hung suspended by small brass chains. My sister Cara dangled in a pouch slung from my mother's shoulders, her baby face closed in sleep. I walked my hands along the edge of the cosmetics case to the perfume testers clustered on a mirrored tray. I sprayed my arms and throat with Blue Grass. I knew the words and expected to be coated with the aroma of grass and oil stuck to the blades of a mower; instead, I smelled like a defunct honeysuckle. I sniffed my forearm closely. The perfume had already dried and penetrated my skin. Now, I suspected, it was coursing through my veins with the blood. The saleswoman leaned over the case and brought her face close to mine. Her skin was pitted and sallow. She wore something sticky on her cheeks and nose. She breathed sour puffs of air. My mother said, Eden! And I froze. But the woman remained hovering over me, smiling like we knew something together. That scared me.

Rita at Saks and I don't share any special knowledge. I get the impression that Rita thinks I'm a bit of a rube. When she dips my credit card into the computer slide and reaches for tissue paper some weariness snags her motions. But I just can't tolerate the idea of trying other counters for someone more sympathetic. Rita's counter is out of the way, and she doesn't mind going to get special things. If Sonny could see me he'd be shocked—or perhaps contemptuous, it's hard to say.

Sonny has been taking me to Scarsdale. In the middle of the night he'll roll from his side of the bed, nestle his face into my neck and say, Are you awake? If I don't have to work the next day, I say yes, and we go off to catch the sunrise over the back nine at the Scarsdale Golf Club. Sonny will be forty in July, and I think this reexposure to Scarsdale is a way of collecting himself before he hands the whole bundle over to middle age. We sit in his blue-gray Toyota banked against the curb before the first house he ever lived in. It is tasteful beyond compare, angled on the irregular slope of grass like a tipped hat. In the early morning light the lawn has turquoise highlights in its erect little blades and the leaded windows each catch a different version of the sun. Sonny doesn't say a lot during these visits, but I can imagine him a toughie with a blond crew cut, pouncing on his little brother Matthew in the backyard. I never pounced on Cara when we were small. Not once.

*   *   *

I leave Rita, carrying a shapely black paper bag dangling from my wrist and walk the few blocks east to the subway in a state of grace. The handsome weight pulls slightly on my arm. My soul feels smooth and settled, but this good feeling vanishes abruptly when I take my seat between two passengers on the packed Lexington Avenue train heading south. My bottom straddles the small plastic hump that allots the true seats.

There is a very young couple diagonally across from me. The man's expression tells me that he has met his companion only moments ago and his greatest desire is to obtain her phone number before his stop arrives. I look to the woman to gauge his chances and am halted effectively by the shape of her eyebrows, which have the exact proportions of boomerangs. Two tiny boomerangs have fixed themselves, midflight, above her startled eyes. This gives her face the aspect of both utter fixity and infinite movement, simultaneously—a powerful combination. I am not surprised at the young man's attraction, but I can't get beyond those brows. I reposition my legs and think of something else. I think of Sonny.

Sonny's been out of town for nearly three weeks now. He's up on Martha's Vineyard where his brother Matthew keeps a summer house. Sonny designs furniture, and when he was first starting out he filled Matthew's house with experiments. Ten years ago a stylist friend used one of Sonny's beds in an ad. The couple in the photograph were eating in the bed and dripping stuff all over the sheets in a way that was meant to be subliminally erotic. The woman didn't actually use her tongue but somehow you kept thinking about it anyway. In New York it became a cult thing to own one of Sonny's beds. Now he doesn't know if he even wants to do furniture anymore. He's taking some time to think over his next move. I believe he's thinking me over, too, and this is a strain. Rita has prescribed something that smells like cranberries to dab on my puffed-up eyes. The bottle is in the bag with lip gel and a nineteen-dollar pair of tweezers.

Just before Sonny left, we sat on our sofa together. He was sketching. I was reading. I leaned over and watched the little half-shape forming on the page. Sonny crosshatched soft shadows on the bowed legs of what looked like a low ottoman.

Fat legs, I said and tapped his arm. But my voice and hand got away from me and what I meant as playful came out slightly vicious, as if his ottoman were ugly or obscene. My tap caused his pencil to slip and a hard black jag pierced the gray curve.

Sonny looked at his ruined drawing, then turned to me and said, Is that better now, Eden?

He put his pad aside and went into the bedroom. I could hear him talking to Matthew on the phone—I knew it was Matthew by the way Sonny was laughing. I held the drawing pad on my lap and tried to rub away the black line, but that just left a scar of white around an indent. Sonny asked Matthew for the ferry schedule to Martha's Vineyard. When I went into our bedroom he was already pushing multicolored T-shirts into a backpack.

Don't do this, I said. Sonny pulled me into his arms and held me. He whispered into my hair. Just a break, he said, just a break. But I think I know an exit when I see one.

I've darted through the crowd at the Twenty-third Street station, but as I head toward my apartment on Eighteenth I slow down. Dinner with Hal is a bad idea. Hal was Cara's boyfriend—he was crazy about her. When Cara started losing her hair from the chemo it got all over Hal's car and then, of course, all over his clothes. He looked like a man with an extraordinary cat, a long-haired chestnut-colored cat.

For a very long time Hal didn't clean his car. One night he picked me up and drove me to the movies on the Upper East Side. The first year was behind us with the first birthday and the first Christmas and all the unexpected days and unexplainable loss, but Hal still had threads of Cara's hair winding through the carpet of his car floor. Twenty minutes into the movie I leaned over and said, I have to go to the bathroom. Then I walked straight out of the theater. All the way home I plucked hairs from my sweater. I couldn't bring myself to drop them on the sidewalk so I put them in my pocket. At home I found a small blue scarf in my dresser to save them in, but when I looked in my pocket it was empty.

That was a year and a half ago, and now, like Sonny, I need to think of my next move. New York doesn't hold me the way it once did. I could go anywhere really—I could even go to Paris for a while. I'm doing a book on Basquiat, which I could do anywhere. I think of Cara dancing. She would roll her closed fists one over the other in counts of three, then on the fourth beat she would stick her thumb out like an arbitrary hitchhiker. This was her only dance, but she could do it to any rhythm. I used to imitate her and laugh until my stomach knotted. Now I catch myself, sometimes, tumbling my fists one over the other and hope the thumb, like a dowser's stick, will point me in the right direction.

There are two messages on my machine, both from Hal. Meet you at Tomoe Joe's at eight sharp, says the first. The "sharp" is a joke; Hal lives in a time warp. The second is: Meet you at Angelica's. No time specified. I like Angelica's.

You look great, Eden, really great. That's what Hal is saying but he can't see me because he's ducking under the archway to get to my booth. Hal is six feet four inches tall. When he bends to kiss me he has to curve his torso low. Hal fits himself into the bench across the table and places his hands on either side of the silverware. His whole body has come to rest. Only his eyes remain scurrying pinballs of gray. If I didn't know him this would be alarming but soon he'll ease into a slower speed and take me in.

Eden, you really do look great. He gives me a brief forehead-to-waist inspection and then stops. In that moment we share an interior catalog, the exact calibrations by which my every feature varies from Cara's. The small jolt at similarities, the huge, irrational disappointment at differences, a curve in the lip, a softer chin. This inventory and its sorrows takes a tenth of a second, and then it's over. Hal is spreading the paper napkin across his knees and the waitress wants to know what we'll have to drink.

Soon the waitress drops a pair of wet-looking screwdrivers in thick tumblers on our table. Hal sips the top off his and says, So, how's Sonny?

I'm wishing I'd gotten some nail polish from Rita.

Disaffected, I say.

What do you mean "disaffected"?

I mean sexually.

Hal sputters. I've said this partly to rattle him. He coughs and says, Christ, Eden. Then a flick of clear-eyed calculation passes across his face before we both recoil and bury our mouths in our drinks. Hal surfaces first. He says, Men are different. It's more a visual thing.

He takes another long swallow and signals the waitress, You look great, he says, Sonny's totally fucked up.

Right after the funeral, the three of us—Sonny, Hal, and I—drove out to Matthew's house on Martha's Vineyard. Hal twisted into the backseat of the Toyota and said, I really like it here. When we finally reached the ferry, however, he sprang out like a compressed sponge exposed to water, fulfilling its true and natural dimensions.

The house was dark and cool in the late afternoon as we dumped our bags in the living room. Sonny put the stuff my mother had wrapped—turkey, slices of ham, macaroni salad, lasagne, food people had been bringing to her house for days—he put it all, just as she had wrapped it, into Matthew's tiny icebox. Sonny suggested a walk before the light gave out, but since Hal and I were both tired he went alone.

Upstairs there are four bedrooms off the central hallway. Sonny and I always sleep in the northeast corner, where even in winter we keep the window raised high and let the sound of the waves rock us. I decided to give Matthew's room to Hal. It overlooks the ocean, too, and has the best bed—one of Sonny's first—with a canopy of braided, burnished aluminum and mesh, so delicate and fine it looks like a tossed handkerchief suspended forever just before descent.

It's a big bed, big enough for Hal. He lay down with his shoes on. His eyes were still; he was watching me closely. I sat beside him on the bed and put my hand spread out in the center of his chest.

Hal? I'm not sure what I was asking him. My hand stayed pressing into his chest. His mouth pulled back, he screwed up his eyes, and started to sob. I tried to hold him but his body was coiled. He was slamming his fist into his forehead until I slipped my hand across and he was hitting my palm instead and then he stopped and I was holding him, stroking his back, long, long strokes along the length of his back to soothe him and me. I held him and stroked down his shoulder and arm, across his chest and stomach, cupped his penis, pressed both palms down the length of his thighs. I rubbed his calves and took off his shoes and rubbed his feet and back up his legs again, like I was the first rinse, the first distance his body took from Cara, like I was absorbing whatever of her lay on him into me. We both fell asleep and slept well into the darkness until Sonny woke us and fixed us some supper.

Hal and I have ordered big salads with crispy fried tofu. He has doused his salad with so many dressings it's nearly floating.

Did Sonny tell you about Dorothy? Hal asks with a smile; he has a piece of beet wedged into his front gum that I try to ignore. I envision Dorothy as a sliver-hipped blonde with a family cottage on Martha's Vineyard.

No, I say, who's Dorothy?

Sonny set me up with her. I can't believe he didn't tell you. Huh.

Yeah, she works for him, Hal says. She's great.

I don't know what to say and for some reason I think of those birds I've seen on telephone wires. They arrive like normal birds, flying in with their wings flapping, but when they leave they just drop, it almost looks like they drop straight through the wire.

Well, that's great, I say to Hal.

She's not like Cara, he says.

No, of course not.

Of course not.

Hal and I close Angelica's. I'm a little drunk when I get home. I sink into the white sofa because it has twice the gravitational pull of the rest of the apartment. I can hear Hal fiddling with the lock. I listen for the sweep of the keys across the floor. He'll slide them under the door, then three taps on the buzzer —good-bye. But now he's having some trouble with the lock. I realize he's locking from the inside and that confuses me. I hear his shoes along the floor and I can smell him, he's sweating, but it's still a surprise when he lands his head on my stomach, face down.

Hal, stop, I say and pry his face from my belly. I push a little on his forehead like I'm revolving a huge smooth immovable stone. Get off, Hal, I say.

He sits up on the floor. I'm watching him in the loose light from the neighbor's apartment across the air shaft. He has that flustered expression he gets when he's thinking about something important.

I don't know what to do, he says. And I can see that's true. A lot of Cara's things are still in Hal's apartment. It never occurred to him that a time might come when her stuff would have no place there. Just beyond his head, I notice the light of the answering machine blinking a frantic red.

Hal, press the button, I say.

I can't be a monk, Eden.

Hal, push the button on the answering machine. It might be for you.

Hal turns his body obligingly toward the bookcase and reaches for the machine resting on the third shelf. He squashes the button and Sonny's voice fills the room, Hey, Eden, where are you?

Sonny! says Hal.

I'm at Matt's apartment in the city. Just got here, says Sonny.

Sonny talks in staccato beats on answering machines. It makes the most mundane messages—asparagus, box of linguine, dish soap—sound slightly urgent. I'm so happy to hear his voice I sit up straight on the sofa, but why is he calling from Matthew's apartment? Why didn't he just come home?

. . . going out to Scarsdale, any interest? Call by three and we're off.

I glance at the green digital numbers on my desk clock. It's ten past, and I know not to hope he's running late. Even in the middle of the night he's punctual.

If not, I'll look for you on the terrace at six. Not there? No problem, bye.

I sink back into the sofa and consider my options. I could ask Hal to drive me out there. I could take the 5:06 train from Grand Central—I did this once before with Sonny when the car lost its muffler. Or I could not go at all.

I decide on the train. Hal stretches out on the sofa for a nap while I get ready. He insists on taking me at least as far as Grand Central. I haven't seen Sonny for a while, and I want to make a good impression. I douse my eyes with half the bottle of cranberry stuff and then I set to work on my brows hoping to shape them into coy arches as compelling as the woman's on the subway, if not quite as dramatic. I'm tweezing away and before I know it I've removed the entire outside half of my right eyebrow. Now I look lopsided and weird and I feel a swell of panic. There's something wrong with me.

When Sonny and I first got together, almost a dozen years ago, when I was nearly twenty, he used to say I had the most beautiful face he had ever seen, anywhere. This wasn't remotely true, of course, but he would shift his body until he was leaning his head on both hands looking straight down into my face like a man who'd discovered the presence of a small but perfect mountain range in his own bed. He couldn't take his eyes off what lay ahead.

What lay ahead was this. I should have told him. I should have pulled each finger from his dazzled cheek and whispered: Someday, in this bed, you'll lift yourself up and look at me as you are now and see a sleepy woman, tired from living so stupidly, a spendthrift and miser who doesn't know when to be which. You'll tell me I'm beautiful because that's your habit but I won't believe you believe it anymore and then you'll leave me. I could have told him that. With the concentration of a surgeon I sketch in with a fine brown pencil the shape my eyebrow might have been.

I'm a little early arriving at the Scarsdale Golf Club. I stand on the west terrace of the clubhouse. A regatta of glass ashtrays floats around me, each adrift on its own umbrella table. There is no place to sit that isn't wet. I wonder if this is a joke, someone sounding just like Sonny leaving a message on our machine, someone who knows our habits. I feel slightly seasick looking over the tipsy hills of the golf course and wish I had thought to bring coffee.

I breathe deeply into the space two inches below my belly button. Dead center of the golf course is a dense little grove of trees that serves as a divider between two holes. Tucked into the middle are three deep-plum-colored trees huddled together, their branches so perfectly shaped they look like a giant bonsai. Winding paths of red chipped stones unravel through the grass, a route so circuitous no golfer would take the time to walk it. The stones are matte and soft looking—like wood, but they're rock. I can see where Sonny gets his designs: all his proportions are here at the Scarsdale Golf Club.

The early morning caddies are backing the golf carts up the stiff slope of asphalt, out from the underground garage. I can hear the whir and hum of the toy engines as they line them up against a white rail fence. Now the hills beyond the rails look oddly and abundantly sexual like the green-clad hips and thighs of reclining women.

I'm beginning to think this was a reckless trip, that Sonny won't be coming after all and even if he does it won't help, when a small girl darts across the putting green of the ninth hole. She is wearing a white sundress and a large white bow on top of her head. I can make out the wisp of a brown ponytail trailing out behind. She races around the sand trap and dives into the grove of trees. After a moment I catch a flash of white shimmering beneath the dark branches of the central bonsai.

Over the top of the hill a gold cart rises carrying a man in an orange golf shirt so bright I think he must expect lawless hunters to trickle down from the mountains to the greens. He, too, wheels around the trap and aims straight for the trees. A scar of dark mashed grass follows his progress until he disappears into the grove.

A burst of white crashes through the other side and the tiny girl is running up the tenth fairway, moving very fast for her size. She's halfway up when the golf cart exits the trees and starts to climb. She gains the top faster than seems possible, and I expect her to drop behind the horizon like a white stone tossed into water. Instead she turns and stares down at the cart. (I imagine the stare, I can't see her eyes. Are they blue?) Then she sits abruptly.

The cart keeps aiming right for her. I realize I don't want him to catch her, that I'm frightened. I'm afraid to watch his orange arm swoop out to grab her, and I almost call out—Run, run—even though I have no reason to think she's in danger. The man stops, and instead of some terrible reeling-in she just stands up, smiles, and climbs into the golf cart. They go over the ridge and then they're gone.

I stare out for a very long time half-hoping the little girl will return. I'm thinking maybe they'll just do a loop beyond the hill and then come back. I watch for so long that the sun tops the trees and some trick of morning light makes the trail the cart left fade back into the grass. I feel a sinking loneliness and drop into one of the deck chairs, suddenly very, very tired. I'm thinking about Cara. I've heard people talk about graceful deaths and beautiful deaths, and I've even heard that said about Cara's. It isn't true.

Somehow we all adjusted our vision to see the bald, rail-thin young woman as the same Cara with the sweet profile whose pretty skin in any light begged touching. We couldn't see what any stranger could have told us—and what the doctors, in fact, had been saying as plainly as they knew how.

My mother says, all the time, that Cara died an amazing death, but actually my mother was in the hospital cafeteria with Hal and Sonny when Cara died. Sonny asked who wanted a second cup of coffee. My mother said she wanted to see the card her friend Louise had sent, so I went back to Cara's room to get it.

I walked through the maze of green-tiled corridors in the oldest wing of New York Hospital. I thought Cara was asleep, as we'd left her, I pushed through her door slowly, on tiptoe. As soon as the light from the hall hit her bed she sat up and screamed something incomprehensible, but I knew from the terror in her eyes she was dying. Two nurses and a doctor flew through the door and pushed her down flat and started clamping something onto her already bruised arm while she struggled, and I started yelling, Get the fuck out of here! Leave her alone! until, to my shock, they did.

I stood alone in the middle of Cara's hospital room, which suddenly seemed gigantic, and listened to her breathing hard and shallow. I knew I should go to her and hold her but I was afraid to touch her. I said, Cara, it's okay. But nothing was okay, and I stood in the middle of the room and watched the life fall out of her body.

It wasn't until the signal on the monitor brought the doctors and nurses back that I wedged between them, circled around her bed, and touched her face—Cara's beautiful face, that wasn't beautiful at all anymore.

When we were small—when Cara was big enough to run but not yet in school—we played in our neighbor's woods. Later, a developer would come and arrange split-levels on a horseshoe road, but for some years Mr. McKim's vast five-acre wilderness abutted our own backyard. My mother was loose about boundaries. Our town was a safe place, she thought, and we could be trusted to stay away from speeding cars.

Cara and I knew trails in the woods that led to different spots of interest: an odd mound of black dirt piled enormously high, and the orchard with its sour, knobby fruit on the other side of a thicket. I was bigger than Cara and could run faster. Sometimes I took off ahead into the woods until she lost sight of me and called out, Eeed? Eeed?

Some perversity in me would wait until I heard the edge of tears wobbling in her voice, Eeed? Only then would I tear back through the woods, running not on the trail but in the wild shortcuts, pushing through brambles and sticker burrs to get to her. I would land suddenly before her like a superhero and sweep her into my arms. I wasn't all that much taller than she—her legs dangled and her feet bumped my calves—but we would cling to each other ferociously for a moment as though we'd just had a very narrow escape. Then I'd put her down, and we'd continue as if nothing had happened. It was just something we did. Now I'm thinking it was a cruel game and a useless one, if games are meant to teach us. When she was really alone I failed to make a critical jump, like some skydiver stalled in an open hatch.

When I spot Sonny stepping lightly along the red stone path winding around the tenth green in the sunshine, I realize I've been crying again. I hate this about myself, crying all the time, and I know without a mirror that mascara has made two black half-moons under my eyes, which look ghoulish. I lick my finger and try to rub away some of the stain as I watch Sonny, little by little, grow bigger on the path. I watch the funny rhythm of his step and the way his face tilts upward as he walks, as though he can absorb all this that he loves, if he can just open himself wide enough. His arms swing loosely at his side and anyone can see he's a happy man, or at least a good one. When I stand up from the white iron deck chair, the whole back of my dress is wet with dew. I pull the fabric away from my legs, walk to the edge of the terrace, wave my arm, and start down the long steep flight to the fairway.

Roundup

A PERFECT MORNING. PHILIP WATCHES GUNNER OVER the top of new titanium reading glasses and wonders just how much it will cost to spray the apple trees. Gunner's got a squirrel trapped. Gunner has teeth like raisins but the squirrel doesn't know that and quivers, freezes on a low branch. A sweet pink blossom shakes to bursting right above its quaking noggin. Freedom just a scramble away. Philip laughs, stupid squirrel.

Philip made the drive to the New London Ferry from the Upper East Side in two and a quarter hours. Babied the Voyager out of the safety zone of seventy. At seventy-five the whole steering column starts to shimmy. At eighty, all is calm. On a good day, it takes Lucy over three hours. But he knows how to bob and weave. He can handle a tremor without freaking out. And here's his reward, the first, freshest cup of joe out of the dockside urn. Lucy thinks she'll make it up by dinner time. Their daughter, Edith, has a full day at school. His girls will play cards on the train.

Gunner is whining. Philip crushes his paper cup in one fist, shoots it into the open construction Dumpster in the drive. Come on, Killer. Gunner runs to him and laps at Philip's bare knees. Gunner really stinks. He's been rooting in the Hendersons's garbage again. Some green stuff coats his teeth. Philip gets a good grip on Gunner's collar. He keeps his nose away from Gunner's smelly breath. Gunner, Gunner, Philip growls and gives him a quick light whack between the ears, just a warning. Lucy would freak out if she saw it. But that's the problem with Gunner, he gets away with everything. And Philip feels helpless to change that because Gunner is old. Long ago, Lucy found him in a deserted lot below Canal Street, a little cocoa Labrador puppy with a broken hind leg—a beautiful baby hunting dog tossed out of someone's Mercedes for peeing on the seat. That's what Lucy said. And it was a story they stuck with. Philip gives Gunner a good rubdown with a paper napkin, disintegrated lettuce clots up Gunner's chocolate fur.

Can't help yourself, can you, he croons now. Philip is a softy: yes, his wife and daughter work him like a puppet. He likes this thought of being navigated by the females in his world. He dangles his hands puppet-style and lifts them mock unwillingly. You and me, boy, he says to Gunner, his unwilling hand yanking Gunner's choke collar. A pair of pushovers. The squirrel, of course, has vanished, out of the tree, out of the yard. And that irritates more than it should.

* * *

Back in the city it's all still there. The printers, the desks they built from salvage, the air conditioner, the partner's wife's blue bookcase and her odd, odd painting on the wall. What's gone, finally, is the partner, thank god. And that removal has cost five thousand dollars so far, on paper. Even though it's Fatty's, his own cousin's, law firm. Something they'd have to discuss. But the expense is ultimately a write-off. Even when the partner pays it.

And the office key will be delivered on Monday morning to Philip's personal bank officer by bonded courier. No pussyfooting around with FedEx. The bank officer was a nice touch. Here was a guy willing to freeze all the partnership assets on Philip's say so. There's a dispute, said Philip, and shazam. It was very satisfying and Fatty had been impressed. Three months ago, after Philip "resigned," Fatty said: Go in every night, without fail. Don't break anything, but be sure he knows you've been there. Haunt him. Leave clues. If he changes the locks, we'll fuck him from here to Kansas. Fatty should be a fortune-teller!

Lucy's student served the papers for half the usual fee, glued the documents to the door with some kind of industrial adhesive that tore off the paint in strips. *And* shot the papers through the mail slot. *And* delivered them to the artist-wife's studio just in case his partner was loafing there. Obsessive student. Now Philip would have to spend an afternoon repainting the office door. But it was all worth it.

The idea of planting another student with a camera was fun, but too expensive. Lucy was for it, pleaded academic value, said: Just the type she'll be dealing with later on. Deadbeat, greedy ingrates. Users. The world is full of them. And she would know. Lucy teaches psychology at Columbia. But Philip calmed her down, saying, Let's not go overboard.

Sometimes Lucy likes to be excessive. When they finally closed on this house, Philip took the Jacuzzi out first thing. He could already picture careless bubbles slopping over the lip, seeping into the joists beneath the marble tiles. There'd be buckling in the subfloor and maybe mold. He'd have to tear the whole bathroom apart, better to nip it in the bud. He thought Lucy would freak out, but she didn't.

Okay, she yawned, You're the architect. A phrase his partner often used in jest. In mockery? Philip could never be sure. His partner had that Midwestern negative-space where a facial expression should be. They were both architects, after all. Even if Philip was senior in all ways. So when Lucy said this—You're the architect —out of the blue, and right in the beginning of all the trouble, Philip watched carefully as her eyes blinked and closed.

No. No sarcasm intended, as far as he could tell. Her face lay on a new satin pillowcase. Her mouth, glistening with Vitamin E, puffed out as if waiting for a kiss. He did kiss her and she mewed in appreciation. He leaned over her shoulder, licked a finger and popped the wick on the jasmine candle.

Lucy would have liked a Jacuzzi, and the lily-of-the-valley bath salts she bought to celebrate still hovered near the place where the tub used to be. But Philip found the pinhole in the seal that would cause all the problems. And a client had some excess blue granite to sell cheap. Now a small stone wall—the kind so valuable around here when it traced pointlessly through a neighbor's wood—was temporarily erected between the toilet and the hole where the tub had been. Philip would lay it himself, a blue stone floor to offset the cool simplicity of white standard fixtures. Now the pink Jacuzzi, with its spun fiberglass undercoat, lay tipped in the driveway like a seashell.

The portable phone rings from somewhere out in the yard, shrill and urgent. Finally he locates it under the picnic table. He'll kill Gunner, who'll know once and for all that the phone is not a toy. Philip lies down on the dew-soaked redwood bench and reaches into the grass beneath. His back gives warning tingles as he straightens up. Lucy's cell-phone number glows in the readout. He deliberates whether or not to answer. She doesn't like it when he drives so fast; he doesn't like to listen to lectures. He'll call her in a half hour to check in.

Philip carries the damp thing back up to the front porch where he'd put it in the first place, where Gunner now naps in a pool of morning sunlight. Philip will read the paper later. He's tired of the paper. Tired of all the big questions. What ever happened to local politics? And what about lust? Katie at Kinko's hadn't flashed a thigh in weeks. The phone shrieks again. Gunner rolls over the porch ledge and gallops off toward the Hendersons's pond. Law- suit, Philip can see it now. Lucy's number glares again in the readout. She won't give up.

Yes, he says, snapping on the phone switch. Yes, a call-waiting yes, taking a disruptive call in the middle of something important. The yes that says: This is an expensive intrusion.

Lucy's voice falters for only a moment: Is that you, Kitty cat?

Yes.

Do you have another call?

After a pause he says, What is it, Lucy?

It's Edith.

Edith?

She has pinkeye.

Oh god.

And I think the discomfort has made her a little aggressive.

What are you talking about?

She knocked a first grader off the magic snail and then sat on his head.

She sat on his head?

Yes, he made fun of her.

Well then.

So, she's suspended now, and contagious.

What do you mean contagious?

What does contagious usually mean, Philip?

Lucy is freaking out. The school nurse was sick herself and the substitute is barely a student!

Take a breath, Lucy, Philip says, Okay?

The student nurse said it could be viral! And the headmaster said Edith is becoming antisocial!

Fuck him.

Philip, sweetheart, please.

Philip listens to Gunner growling somewhere. Did you try Benjami?

Benjami is the family doctor, also second cousin once removed of Philip's and of Fatty's. They all used to share the same surname before Philip shortened his to Ben. Philip Ben. Sounds like a very nice watch, Fatty said. Lucy and Edith are Twitchells. Edith was born in a brief moment when women like Lucy were thinking matrilinealy. Philip doesn't care. Though the Benjamis do. All of them never mention it. But they are vocal about Gunner's discipline problems, and now Edith's would be communal property, too. Mixed marriage. That's the trouble. Nothing could be plainer.

The central mouthpiece on this is Fatty's wife, leaky-lips Arden. Talk, talk, talk. But even after birthing four sons, she's as beautiful as ever, really causing problems for her husband—sweet problems, problems of driving off the lust of his friends. No one troubles Philip on this front, and he feels a moment's irritation. Feels there was something his cousin Fatty should know: the delicate, gorgeous, subtle but flamboyant superiority Philip enjoys—but to explain would somehow compromise it. Look at this property, Fayad Benjami. In Quoin, Connecticut! As soon as the renovations are done: a family gathering, in the garden, in the orchard, with lobsters!

Philip? Honey? That phone is on the fritz.

The New London train station with its brick facade and waterside arcade is a tender meeting place, but Lucy has elected to take the bus. The one o'clock sun presses hard on Philip's head, two ferry rides have given him a pink spot where the hair is finest. He shields this with his hand and waits while Gunner pants, tongue lapping over the rim of the open back window of the Voyager.

Dick's Fish Fry doubles as a bus depot. It's so hot the outdoor lunch crowd appears to wobble in their seats. An oily smell that seems bad for everyone's arteries carries on the wind. He can taste the greasy cod at the back of his throat. He's not going to worry about this. He ignores it. He can just do that. Lucy likes to say that Philip's sensibilities are exquisite. She says this with a shrug to fend off the potential jealousy of her listener. Over many a boiled dinner with Lucy's family his bludgeoned senses were acknowledged with mostly silent approval. He'd eat the carrots and push all that odd striated meat to the side.

That's what you get for marrying a black man, said Lucy's grandmother, A lot of nonsense and rigamarole.

Philip's not black, Nana.

My eye, he's not.

And there was that shrug.

There is so much he could be doing right now. So much it irritates even to think about it, so he counts the number of gray-blue Corollas in the parking lot and that satisfies something, some need to know things, but what or why he can't be certain.

The bus is later than usual. Gunner curls down for a nap.

At last, at last, here at last! Their very own jitney, Lucy likes to say. And now that it finally swivels into place Philip agrees, it *is* very shiny and tall. A pleasant pneumatic sound to the brakes, the doors sweep open, Philip grins, genuinely happy they've arrived. But as always his smile wilts by the time Lucy manages to gather the infinite number of parcels and objects she's brought along on the trip.

Part of the freedom of having a country house is that you can travel unencumbered. Just leave the city behind and turn the key in your own special paradise. No packing required. This had been less true with their Sag Harbor house perhaps, because they'd rented it out so often, so lucratively.

Still, now, something in Lucy rebels. She hovers in the bus's deep disembarkation cavity, marshaling her mother's vintage Louis Vuitton hat cases and some half-torn bags from Gristedes. Philip should rush forward to help. But he has the thought, like a déjà vu, that it's better if she struggles with the consequences. Though twelve years of such struggle has failed to correct the problem so far.

Gunner howls at the sight of her. Howls and cries at his saviour. Reenacting, as he always does during any reunion, his memory of despair in the sad, deserted, below-Canal-Street lot: Tossed from a luxury vehicle and abandoned! Until Lucy found him! And gave him her home!

And Lucy howls back, adjusts two slipping embossed circlets on her forearm and croons. Philip doesn't need to turn his head to gauge the rapt attention of the lunch crowd. He can feel it soak into his bandanna neckerchief along with the fish fry. He examines with care the way the salt air is drying up his cuticles, so quickly! while Lucy hefts her load onto the boiling pavement. Clearing the way for Edith. His little girl. Here she is. Dressed in a darling pink gingham dress and Philip's brand new three-hundred-dollar UVB-screening sunglasses. No wonder he couldn't find them. Edith presses into his arms for a hug, her cheek against his chest, and to his credit he never once thinks: Contagious.

Pure luck squeezes them onto the ferry at the last second before the chain gets dragged across the aft deck. The ferry groans away from the dock while a string of black and silver and white German-made cars rev along the shoreline. Nothing for them but the stink of fuel in the breeze. Philip was right to buy American. When his partner found that old Porsche— so cheap, such low mileage, no rust!—his partner said, Let's make it the Official Vehicle. What better way to say form and function?

He pronounced it *foam auction*. Some lack of emphasis or articulation. This, like so much else, bugged Philip. But by the time Philip was through with him, he'd be *living* in the rust-free collectible. His artist wife will really get into *that*. Philip laughs out loud.

Lucy turns to see what the hell could be so funny. Edith is doubled over, head between her adorable sunburned knees. Seasick? Philip mouths. They've barely left the cove.

Lucy's eyes looks grave. Here's Philip enjoying a private joke, and now from the back of the Voyager, Gunner warms up for a croon.

Gunner, please, I'm begging you, whispers Lucy. And Gunner lifts his muzzle, laps back the yelp.

Good boy, Lucy sighs, leaning back. Good, good boy.

Edith folds into Lucy's lap, her delicate shoulder blades heave convincingly, authentically, under the pink and white checks of her sundress. Lucy strokes the pale tips of Edith's braids. Philip hopes she won't vomit on his sunglasses. And instantly hates himself: he's a horrible person, unworthy of all his good fortune and talent. Just a total crap of a human being. Fatty always said so, but that was in jest, back when Fatty had a sense of humor. And only after Philip had plied him with too much food and drink. Like at the end of the nice farewell to Sag Harbor dinner.

You're a dick, Fatty raised a tumbler of vodka and lime. To the biggest dick of them all. Fatty had crab meat stuck in his teeth.

But who was Fatty to be casting any big stones? Hadn't it all been his idea? *Look at the lease,* said Fatty, like an oracle. Just look at the lease! And he had, they both had, and they thought hard about Edith's unexpected crawl. Straight over the "patio" and into the square of cement they euphemistically called the "lily-pond" but which could readily be reinterpreted as the "pool."

What a scene! His darling, barely nine months old, tumbling forward into a miniature, but still *watery* expanse unprotected by a fence. That Lucy pounced on Edith in a heartbeat was beside the point. Fatty negotiated the settlement and the transfer of title. And Philip became a homeowner with his very first summer rental. A fabulous coup just when Philip was considering his options. It was a dry spell for architects; several colleagues were already waiting tables. The house was a bomb, but a lousy house on a desirable block. Where better to turn his talent and attention? Really an astonishing bit of luck.

But that was before Fatty became a purist. Philip hadn't been called a dick for a while now. He misses all that. He should call

Fatty, today, without delay. Because Fatty is depressed and losing focus. And if they're not careful the rewards of partnership dissolution may slip away. Yes, Fatty is preoccupied. But he does have Philip's sympathy in what sounds like a big mix-up.

Tunisian, they are Tunisian. Tunisian-American. Fatty and Philip both born in Jersey City. But when the second roundup happened, something abstract and surprising, something buried deep in the newspaper, Fatty's own son, Jamal, was stopped by a classmate, an ROTC recruit, and escorted to the Student Life Office. A small tired man asked to see Jamal's identification. Jamal, a spoiled boy, really a worry to his mother, chuckled. His birthday was soon. The man with the sad gray eyes had been hired by his friends to tease him.

The man asked again. Jamal offered a defunct Blockbuster Video card, playing along. Since that day the college has been very accommodating. There's even an offer on the table to overlook a poor showing in macroeconomics. A new beginning. His parents have been told that Jamal was very, very helpful the two weeks he was detained. Something that surprises them, that gives them a peculiar disembodied hope, like a dream under sedation. But nothing can shake the disturbance of the strange interlude—it's physical now, Fatty says, in the esophagus, he can't swallow—in which their deeply unfocused, undisciplined boy was held just in case he might participate in something intricately organized.

Can't swallow. That's what Fatty says every time Philip calls. He needs to call Fatty today. He will. And now it looks like

Edith has fallen asleep. And if he soaks the sunglasses in ammonia, it will clean them better than new. What was he worried about? He's sorry. And moves closer to his wife and child. Curls over them on the wooden bench. Should he fetch some water?

Lucy shakes her head. Right away Philip can tell Edith knows, subconsciously, that her father is on the job. All difficulties are behind them, left on shore. Her heaving shoulders—tiny fluttering tips of angel's wings—have slowed to a gentle rise and fall. A sleeping girl in her mother's lap. Lucy closes her eyes like she might doze now as well, her hand cups lightly over the lacy bow of Edith's dress. She tips her own face up into the breeze. Philip will find some water anyway, just in case.

Back at the house, Lucy gently pries Edith, fast asleep, from beneath the seat belt. She slings their daughter over one shoulder, smiles to Philip to communicate the delicious heaviness of their delicate child. But the heat pouring from Edith's skin worries her, cancels the smile. Lucy fans Edith with her free hand, elbows open the screen door, and makes it inside. Philip lets Gunner go. Gunner circles up to bump against the screen door then back down and around until his hind side disappears into the Hendersons's azalea. Philip decides to assess the newspaper after all, on the cool of the porch.

Minutes later, Lucy has changed her clothes. I have a present for *you,* she smiles. She rocks one hip against the screen door, makes it squeak. Her linen pants, cropped to reveal thin ankles, are a spider web of wrinkles from being crammed into a hat case. But the color is as pale as the blue of her eyes and in this springtime afternoon light her skin looks soft and pretty. Pretty girl, Philip hums. Come 'ere pretty girl, and hollows out his lap, moves the paper to the floor.

Right here, you. He eases off his reading glasses and glances around for the case. Lucy stays where she is, both hands, he notices, tucked behind her back. Whatcha got there, vixen-bride?

A present.

A present, eh? Well, check out this present. In truth, there isn't much for her to check out, but he shifts around as if there is and she laughs and looks over her shoulder into the house, blushes, and shrugs. The shrug that says Edith will sleep fitfully and be upon them. By Philip's reckoning Edith has been sleeping fitfully for a decade now.

He nods, grins, Whatcha got? And crosses his legs slowly, tightly, sexily, he thinks, and Lucy teeters in the doorway, pink with pleasure. They can make each other happy this way, just making believe. Well?

This. Lucy tugs at something in a big Gristedes bag. Don't freak out, she says.

Who's freaking out? But then he spots what she has in her hand. It's the painting! That weird, sick painting he's forced to look at whenever he stops by the office. His partner hung it up right after Philip's "resignation." (Don't ever, ever say that word out loud, Fatty said.) And there it was—bugged maybe? —each time Philip went in to the office at night to check up. To read things, to watch for new invoices, new proposals, to make sure the equipment was still there, to download new designs onto his laptop. He couldn't, obviously, take sets of drawings, but who needed to? He'd found the original lease, and the corporation issuance. It was his right. He could take anything he wanted until the corporation was dissolved. With Fatty's checklist, he'd found it all, easily. His partner is an idiot who doesn't know what to hide. For a long time, the dope didn't even get his own lawyer. When Fatty said, don't worry, he'd act as "mediator" for the breakup, Philip's partner failed to understand that was just a colloquial expression.

And the painting. That strange blob on the wall reminded him of why it was good to be doing what he was doing. What people got famous for these days. Fame used to mean something. But the artist wife wasn't rich and she wasn't pretty, and apparently, Lucy whispered, she was having a rough time getting pregnant. Good thing she has her art, Lucy laughed, but only a little because Edith's conception hadn't been all that easy.

Fuck, Lucy.

What?

You know what.

But she doesn't, and he doesn't either, entirely. Though he suspects this is a big problem and needs to get a hold of Fatty right away for damage control. Just wrap it up. Don't break it whatever you do.

Me? Break it?

Yes, you, Miss Two Left Hands. Just put it down. Find me the phone.

That painting, that blob, was worth twenty thousand at least. He'd attended the wife's last opening, when things were still cordial, when she wore a support stocking as a dress and refused to speak English. He remembered all the nonsense about the *personal* painting, something too intimate to be sold. That small blue mess had required safekeeping from all the waving checkbooks. And sure enough there it was in Lucy's unreliable grasp. Maybe if Philip left right away, he could return it to the office wall before anyone was the wiser. Lucy! Wake up! Go, go, go!

All the happy flush gone, Lucy sets the painting down then slinks out into the long grass following Gunner's trail. He notices her posture isn't all it once was and that makes him sad on top of everything else.

Daddy, what's Mummy doing?

She's getting the phone, princess.

The phone is in the pond?

Yes, darling, that's where Gunner put it.

Oh, Gunner.

Umm. Let me see you. Did you sleep in those sunglasses? Philip thinks the left side stem looks bent. Edith's crumpled dress, the haywire sunglasses, her high blonde braids frayed like rope. Sweetie, what have you done with yourself?

Maybe Mummy needs some help? Edith sticks out a shockingly filthy finger, as if she, too, has been raiding the Hendersons's garbage. She plunges this brownish finger behind the tilted lens of Philip's sunglasses and rubs vigorously.

Stop! Stop!

The finger freezes. Her whole body freezes in its gentle collapse against the door frame. Philip takes a moment to observe: if she continues this way she'll end up like her mother, stooped and prone to excess.

Give me your hand, he says, and feels good about the tone: light, but in command. He'll have her dimpled fist away from the infection and dipped in something antibacterial in no time. He'll fix her hair and her dress while he's at it. But just as he's lifting himself out of the captain's chair, Edith shrieks, finger ricocheting away from her—now Philip can see—*pustulant* eye. His three-hundred-dollar sunglasses fly into the gravel.

Mummy's drowning! Mummy's drowning! Edith is hysterical. She leaps off the porch, lands in the white gravel with a crunch, and speeds through the long grass, off into the low azalea to the Hendersons's fetid pond. Philip hears the crackle, of course, of his sunglasses beneath her foot. Why even bother to look.

He makes his way, casually, behind her. Freaking out; his

girls are on constant high alert. And he is just their slave boy, following along to do their dirty work, to clean up the daily mess: emotionally, mentally (Lucy could barely get through *Chicken Soup for the Soul* without his exegesis), physically—here he comes—and spiritually, his taming influence was evanescent and constant. The Hendersons's pond was two feet deep. The frogs couldn't get enough depth to spawn.

Sweetheart, he calls. Honey bun, he sings out tiredly, Mummy's fine. He kicks aside the azalea and makes the turn on the path to the pond. Love bug? His forward foot snags, catches him in a tangle of cattails, and there, just ahead, is Lucy facedown in the water and motionless.

Oh my god, oh my god, and if he could run he certainly would. He thinks, many times, a stuck and flickering reel in his tired head, I'm coming. But it is Edith who pounces on her mother, straddles Lucy's back like a tiny fierce boxer, yanks her mother's head, nose, and mouth above the surface, and slams her fist hard between the shoulder blades to strike out the suffocating water.

And in this way, hair held in her daughter's fist, neck arched, Lucy chokes on the first renewed breath. She heaves and chokes. Edith lets go. Lucy's head lurches forward into the water again. Face under, with some strength somewhere, she tries to shake her daughter off her back. But Edith presses a cheek down hard against her mother's in tandem. If Lucy insists on drowning, Edith is going to too.

*   *   *

Later, Jack Henderson tells Philip he lifted up the phone without thinking, before putting on his glasses to really make sense of the scene from his second story study. He tries to link this reflex to a brief patch with the Navy SEALs after Harvard, but no one is listening. Long before Philip untangled himself, the plaintive squeal of the ambulance was getting louder, coming to them.

Now Lucy and Edith sit entwined on the Hendersons's antique rattan recliner. Lucy wears Nonnie Henderson's tennis sweater over snug pink sweat pants. And Edith is wrapped like an enormous infant in a blue down comforter. The police are long gone. And the emergency team. Lucy fainted, nothing more. She, too, has something vaguely viral, that and forgetting to eat, or sleep. She just fainted, face down, in the water.

There'd been a hammy round of applause for Edith, whose timing, it turned out, had been miraculous. Now the heroine shivers against her mother's sporty chest, while Nonnie Henderson fusses with the teapot. Philip isn't even thinking about suing over this, he still feels a clammy sweat behind the ears, between his shoulder blades, and he's pretty sure Jack Henderson won't sue, either. He seems relieved, not litigious. In fact, this might give Gunner a free ride, too. They can all start fresh as neighbors. What a good idea.

*   *   *

For a tiny, happy moment, amnesty and forgiveness seem to glow around the painting as well. Maybe Philip can forget he ever saw it, leave it to his partner to sort out. Who knows who goes in and out of that office? But Fatty is emphatic: Are you crazy? Take it back. Now. This minute.

Fatty's one to be talking about minutes. All afternoon and all evening Philip left messages with Jamal, who still hasn't gone back to college. (A disgrace, his mother is destroying his character.) And when Fatty finally decides to lift up the phone he can't stop yelling. You've lost your senses! Entirely! I mean completely! This is an *enormous* problem, Fatty shouts. And Philip understands.

The family never criticizes Lucy directly, but never praises her, either. Jealousy, Philip has always believed. Lucy's family came over on the *Mayflower* or some related vessel very soon after; Fatty's and Philip's papas flew over on Pan Am. But now he wonders, as he aims the Voyager through the hot sticky night down I-95. He wonders if they are right to think what they never say about Lucy.

Philip never wanted his own practice. Never wanted a partner. Never, now that he thinks about it, wanted to be an architect. Long, long ago, he did want to fuck Lucy Twitchell. And that small, simple, natural desire had led to so many half-choices guided by her mindless half-notions. Here he is, careening over the Triboro Bridge to undo, once again, some tangled mess generated by his overzealous wife. Maybe Fatty is right. Certainly Fatty was right about one thing: the Quoin house, like nearly everything they own, is in Philip's name. Lucy can hurl her entire inheritance at it, she'll never get it.

Just before midnight, Philip circles down into the spiral entrance to the garage beneath their apartment building. He wakes Jesus, flat out in a deep snooze on a cot in the underground cubicle. Jesus, it turns out, has "sublet" Philip's private parking space. But Philip will take anything now and tosses the keys. As a goodwill gesture, he tells Jesus he won't report him, and starts the climb back up the ramp. The office is right around the corner. Something Lucy pleaded for; she wanted him close to home. What if Philip had to work nights and weekends?

But as it happened he never did work nights, or weekends either. He was fixing up the house in Quoin. He only had two hands! And early on, after the first month or so, he explained to his partner, fairly patiently, that what Philip did wasn't about *time spent,* it was about the *quality* of his input. And he got Fatty's accountant to explain the same thing. *Intellectual* property. Philip had the brains, the influence, the connections; his partner did the grunt work: designs, drawings, proposals, and such, which took a lot of time no matter how you sliced it. *And* Philip put up the larger share of the start money. Nearly three thousand dollars! To his partner's lousy two grand. And when his partner said "sweat equity," Fatty made a good joke, said,

Let him sweat before a judge. Basically, his partner was an employee whom Philip had made the crazy mistake of treating as an equal.

It happens, Fatty had sighed, and now he'll buy you a swimming pool. Yes, it looked entirely possible that for all his pain and suffering Philip would be rewarded with the inground kidney-shaped pool he'd always dreamed of, in Quoin, Connecticut, right beneath the apple trees. Fatty was a genius, back when he could still focus.

The painting isn't big but it's heavy. Philip adjusts the frame under his arm as he rounds the corner. He fingers the backing, just to check. Maybe there really is a surveillance device. He nudges a gallery sticker. In fact, there's a museum tag, too. Couldn't off-load this pooch, he's thinking when, in his peripheral vision, he catches sight of something that makes his heart lurch. The Porsche! And worse, worse, much worse, the wife sitting in it! He can see her pointy head in the wash of light from the police cruiser pulled in right in front of her.

Philip stops. Ready to spin and bolt, but it's too late. The car door opens and she's out and shouting: You found it! Thank god! Thank god. And she's running to him, arms spread wide like she loves him. And he's paralyzed. He'll think about this later, the way his knees lock and his chest pounds like a thick, dark drum. Oh, she says, coming closer, coming to him, her hands clicking together in an odd way, as if playing small cymbals, small cymbals of joy. He's never seen anyone so happy and he doesn't know what to do.

Was it in the trash?

She's talking to him. Her small angular face tilts up, beaming at him, smiling with square little teeth. Her hand rests on the painting under his arm, but doesn't pull. It's something they're holding together. Something they're protecting. He wonders for a brief half-second if he has some claim here, but then she says, We thought you stole it. I'm so sorry. It was someone else. It's been someone else all along.

I don't know what you're talking about.

Of course you don't. It's late. Go to bed. Go home. I'm so grateful, you'll never know. She stretches up on her small toes and kisses him, a soft delicious wetness just south of his lower lip. There's a sudden hard smell like ammonia. And then she slides the painting out of his grasp, fast and slippery, pulls it away, and he is sick with want. She's done something to him, something awful, but he doesn't know what. Has she infected him? He can't swallow. He tries and tries. Her bitter-smelling little body click-clacks away, away, away, until it's sucked up by the dark of the vestibule. The police officer eyes him slowly, then bangs the cruiser roof with a thick fist, snaps off a barking radio, and follows her inside. His building, his office, his corporation. Come back here! he cries out. Come back this minute! But everything is still and quiet. His knees release with a sudden jerk. He catches himself just before he falls all the way down. He's free to go.

Rome

OLIVIA'S FATHER HAD BLOWN INTO THEIR LIVES, AS HER mother liked to say, just in time for dinner. Olivia's mother was whipping together the odd stuff she'd found in the kitchen: leftover asparagus soufflé—flat, cold, but still good—toasted cheese on whole wheat toast, and lentil soup, reheated. Her mother concentrated on slicing the cheese very thin. She pulled a lighter from her pocket and lit a cigarette. Above their heads, Olivia heard the dull distant pounding of her father's shower. He always showered after the train ride from the city.

Olivia folded her homework and cleared the table. She received a quick smoky kiss from her mother for no reason. Her father came downstairs and into the kitchen, fresh and pink-faced. How's my pumpkin? he said, and kissed her, too. The sleeves of his blue sweater were pushed back to the elbows, and the dark hairs on his wrists still shimmered with dampness.

Olivia's mother had the sandwiches ready to slide under the broiler.

Oh, don't do that, said her father, let's go out. Olivia held his hand, pulling each of his long fingers in succession.

You want to go out? Her mother paused.

Sure, why not? he said. He picked a piece of cheese from one of the sandwiches and popped it into his mouth. Let's go to Nano's, get some antipasto, a little wine. Consider it training.

Her mother slipped the tray inside the oven and closed the door. If we train much more we'll never get there, she said, and laughed three notes like a doorbell. Olivia's father reached over and put his big hands around her mother's waist. He could nearly get his fingers and thumbs to touch, she was that slim. Whatever you say, boss, he said, pulling her close, crushing her blouse, kissing her hair, and winking at Olivia. In a few years, as if in odd defiance of those hands, her mother's waist would expand, pushing outward, farther and farther. Olivia would watch her mother frown in dismay, straining to zip a size-ten skirt. But for now, the winter before Rome, her mother's waist was smaller than Olivia's and getting tinier each day.

Everyone was waiting for Olivia to finish the third grade; then they would move to Rome. The new apartment awaited them, the hallways so long and wide, her father said, that Olivia could bowl. He was happier about moving than her mother. Already he was spending whole weeks away from them, getting Rome ready for Olivia.

Her father let go of her mother. He opened the back door and balanced on the threshold. Looking up into the sky, he took a deep dramatic breath. Her mother shivered in her pale cotton blouse and watched the back of him. A tiny crease formed at the top of her nose. She turned and peeked into the oven, then called over her shoulder, Pete, it's freezing. Olivia will catch cold.

I'm fine, said Olivia.

You know what I was thinking? her father said, closing the door, coming inside. Why don't you and Olivia come into the city on Wednesday, spend the day, do some shopping?

Oh, that's impossible, her mother said. I have at least a half dozen appointments on Wednesday. She sounded slightly puzzled, like they were playing a guessing game.

Well, Olivia could come by herself.

On a school day?

It wouldn't kill her, he said, and drew an imaginary pistol, cowboy-style, and fired at Olivia. Something in her mother's eyes caught Olivia and made her forget to fall over dead.

See? he said, as if his point were proven.

Well, I don't know, her mother laughed again, scratchy and high.

I just thought it might be fun.

Probably it would be. Her mother used a big spatula to lift the sandwiches onto a green and gold dish. She placed it on the table. Get the napkins, angel; her hand brushed the top of Olivia's head.

You're not going to believe this, but I have to go back in tomorrow morning. Christ, this new marketing guy is an ass.

On Saturday?

Her father shrugged and nodded. He picked up Olivia's math homework and smiled.

But you just got here, her mother said. You've been gone for days.

I know. I know. It's crazy.

Her mother watched him for some time, as if he were still talking, then she finally said, Yes, that's exactly what it is. She reached for the soup pot, forgetting the mitt.

On Wednesday morning her mother's face looked clear but tired, aimed at the train tracks ahead. Bells started to ring and safety gates clamored down across the street. The huge train pulled into the station.

Her mother's sudden kiss felt dry and too light, like a dead bug blown across her cheek. Olivia said good-bye in a blur and started running toward the train. She heard her mother call out behind her, Darling, you have plenty of time. But she ran anyway.

The conductor shooed all the boarding passengers to the front of the train. Olivia walked through several cars before she reached the empty seat behind the locomotive. If there was a head-on collision she'd be the first to go, after the engineer.

Olivia pressed her face against the dirty glass pane and then withdrew it slightly. Her mother was looking for her, up and down the train. Bent forward in her ivory coat and off-white stretch pants she looked to Olivia like a big wishbone strained to the limit.

A new driver named Nat was waiting for Olivia when she got off the train. He stood on the platform holding a cardboard sign above his head with *Olivia* written in red Magic Marker. She could see her name rocking back and forth in his hands.

Hello, Olivia?

Where's Boris? she asked when she was close.

He's no longer with us, sorry to say.

Dead?

Nat looked surprised, but he didn't laugh. No, no, he just has a different job now.

The long black car was warm and smelled like eucalyptus when Olivia slipped into the backseat. Nat explained he couldn't allow her to sit in front, as Boris usually did, in case of an accident. Olivia appreciated his sense of danger.

You can never be sure of the other driver, he said. How can you even be sure of yourself? You take precautions, you give it your best shot, what can I tell you?

She liked Nat. She liked the way he made slow wide turns as if he were driving the car in the air. Olivia watched the iced trees of Central Park skitter by. Soon the car came to a halt before the General Motors tower. Sometimes Olivia dreamed her father had the same leaning forward giantness of this building.

*   *   *

It was obvious to Olivia that Ann Marie was a secretary only in passing. She looked more like a fashion model, except she was short. She had lots of black curly hair. She wore a tight black skirt and sweater and very red lipstick. Ann Marie spoke with an accent.

Olivia, what are you becoming now? You are flowering and flowering, I think. She waved a little bird hand at Nat. He nodded to Olivia and vanished down the hushed hall. When the phone rang Ann Marie took the call perched on the arm of the flannel sofa, her short pretty legs crossed. Umm, she said, over and over.

A clatter of voices started up outside. The long hallway was decorated with fake Roman torches hung from fake marble walls. Olivia could see her father at the far end surrounded by people. She wondered if the "ass" was among them. She didn't think her father noticed her yet.

Ah, there he is, said Ann Marie, waving.

Olivia's father came in and hugged Olivia very hard, as if he hadn't seen her in ages, or she had come a long difficult way to find him. She could smell his aftershave, like a saddle just after polishing. Olivia loved that smell, and it made her want to hug her father more, to hug him now, while he was still exactly this way. He let her go and began slapping the pockets of his suit, searching for something important.

Well, what do you think of my girl, Ann Marie? he said, still digging for something, now in the interior pocket of his suit jacket.

She is more and more like her father, I think so.

Oh, really?

Yes, especially the forehead. She paused. Olivia's father smiled; he got the joke. He had an exceptionally wide forehead; it gave him the appearance of being very smart. And the brain behind, this is obvious.

What about beauty, Ann Marie? he said, as though chiding her. But that's her mother's province.

Ann Marie looked down at her perfect hand. She brushed a speck from her fingertip and said, Of course. Then she went outside to her desk without saying anything more.

Her father scattered some papers on his desk, then called to Ann Marie that he and Olivia were going to Bergdorf's. Ann Marie looked up from her desk and grinned unexpectedly. Her red lips made a nice curve, almost like a clown's, Olivia thought.

Well, pumpkin, it's not too inspiring, is it?

Her father surveyed the entire children's department with a kind of weary contempt. Then his eyes widened slightly. Olivia knew he had discovered the precise right thing, something a less skillful shopper would have entirely overlooked. The dress he'd targeted was navy blue with two lines of small, flat silver buttons running down the front. At close inspection it wasn't much different from her school uniform, except that it had a white collar.

What do you think? he said, holding it up against her chest. His eyes darted from the top of her head to her eyes to the dress. He was checking everything to make sure it was just right. Olivia's mother called this "effete," but Olivia knew he was just talented, like an artist. Although she preferred lavender, lavender anything, and her mother always let her get it, her father had decided on the dress with the buttons and was looking for a salesperson.

Just then a woman with long blonde hair, wearing a puffy fur coat, entered the children's area and walked toward them on tippy toes as if she was about to surprise them, though they were looking straight at her. Perhaps I could be of some assistance, she said. Her eyes were blue and large. She seemed to think what she was saying was hilarious.

Wonderful, said her father shaking his head. Something in his voice caught Olivia and made her skin feel strange.

The woman stopped smiling, and Olivia realized she wasn't very old. That's a nice dress, said the woman, but she didn't sound sure.

Don't you ever think? asked her father. He sounded as if he expected an answer. The woman stared, her light eyes enormous and pale like the tips of two blue Popsicles. Olivia looked to her father, who seemed both very interested in this person and, at the same time, not at all—just like football, when he'd hoot through a game, then forget the score.

The woman backed up a step. Her puffy coat caught on a

pair of tiny jodhpurs. She yanked herself loose and dashed toward the elevator; she managed to squeeze through the closing doors at the last second. Olivia's father stuck the dress back onto the rack.

This place is hopeless, he said.

Who was that?

Nobody, said her father, shaking his head and watching the elevator. Really, absolutely nobody.

On the ground floor they passed a jewelry counter. Her father stopped to look. The saleswoman pulled out a pair of circular earrings made of ivory. He picked one up.

Looks like a Life Saver, said Olivia.

Well, we don't need that, said her father and replaced it on the velvet mat. He pointed to a little gold horse with ruby-chip eyes. The saleswoman retrieved it. Olivia's father pinned the horse to the collar of Olivia's coat. The saleswoman beamed.

What a father you have! she said.

Olivia shrugged, embarrassed, then immediately felt her father's irritation, his disappointment in her.

My daughter is a mime, he explained to the saleswoman. She had gray hair near her ears but giggled like a teenager. Her voice sparkling and high for such an austere face. Oddly, it was this woman Olivia would remember, this woman's manicured hand running through silvery curls, long after her father had moved from Rome to Cairo.

79

The saleswoman took Olivia's father's credit card. As an afterthought, he selected the panda by the same designer and nodded. The earrings remained on the mat. The saleswoman packaged the panda and gave Olivia's father his card back. He handed Olivia the small box and said, Give this to your mother. Which was rewarded with another wave of approval from the saleswoman. Then they were pushing out the revolving door. Olivia followed the soft gray cashmere of her father's coat pressed against the glass.

On the sidewalk it was just beginning to snow.

How about some hot chocolate, muffin? her father asked. Olivia was ambivalent about this nickname. She loved it because of her father, but feared it referred to her physically, that her face or her body resembled a muffin in some way. Her father rifled in his pocket and took out a sheaf of green bills.

It seems preposterous for you to come all this way and go home empty-handed, sweetheart. I think that blue dress was a hit. He handed her the money, You go back and pick it up while I get us set up for a snack.

He pointed in the direction of the Plaza Hotel, about a hundred feet away. Olivia knew where he meant. They always went to the Palm Court. But she'd never been allowed to go anywhere in New York alone before. Her father must be making a mistake that he would realize in a moment. But he patted her back toward the revolving door and said, You're going to be a city girl soon, you know. And once she was moving inward, within her slice of glass, he was gone.

She passed the jewelry counter and waved to the woman but without her father the woman didn't seem to see her. On the third floor again Olivia picked up the navy blue dress with the two lines of flat silver buttons. She was nervous at first, but then she realized she liked shopping by herself. Her father was teaching her something. He was preparing her for Rome. She brought the dress to the salesman and handed him all the money. He gave her an enormous amount of change. It never occurred to her that she might have chosen anything she wanted.

On the street it was snowing harder now. The daylight was gray and dim but the Plaza lights were bright. The doorman's booth glittered like a fortune-teller's at a carnival. She knew her father was waiting for her, but Olivia felt a strong undertow of hesitation.

Across the street, directly before her, like a front yard for the Plaza, was a little square with a huge fountain. Because it was February there was no water shooting out. A painter huddled in the cold, his canvases perched against the fountain's parapet. Olivia crossed against the light and walked carefully up and down before the paintings, adopting her father's shopping attitude. Nothing jumped out at her.

Are you looking for anything special? asked the man. He stayed seated, and though he seemed young, his eyes looked stripped of color. Olivia thought making all those paintings had been a strain. She tried harder to find something she could appreciate. Olivia bent to examine one small canvas, a dark sea of muddy squares touched all over with bits of white and gold, something to keep the squares from going under. She asked the artist what the painting was called.

Dawning Day, twenty dollars.

Olivia decided she would show her father and if he liked it they could buy it together. She was excited now and ran through the stand of taxis to the Plaza.

The maitre d' recognized Olivia and smiled. They always sat at the same table. Her father's gray coat was draped on the usual chair back. There was a shivery-looking highball, nearly finished, and a squat silver pot on a doilied plate, but her father wasn't there. Olivia slid into the upholstered chair. The maitre d' held it for her, then pushed her in toward the table. The violinist smiled his plaintive smile. Tilting his violin toward his cheek, he began to play something that elves might play if they were having a good day. Olivia looked around for her father.

Through the door she could see the light turning purple outside. She looked toward the main lobby with its display cases of heavy jewels hung like paintings on the walls. There, Olivia spotted the top of her father's dark head. She was intensely relieved, but afraid he might be angry with her for taking so long.

Maybe he was searching for her. She waved to catch his attention, but his back was turned, and he was mostly hidden by a potted palm. She pushed back the extremely heavy chair and went over to the border of the Palm Court and was squeezing between two plants when all of her father came into view, and the person he was talking to.

The blonde woman in the fur coat from Bergdorf's leaned against the jewel case. Thick diamonds hovered behind her head like a crown, but she looked hurt, puffy-eyed. Olivia's father passed his large hand over the woman's cheek and held it there, completely obscuring her face from Olivia.

Olivia slipped back between the palms to their table. The waiter came over and poured her cocoa. He dropped three marshmallows into the top of her steamy cup. The orchestra played a polka. Then the violinist took a break, standing behind a partial screen sipping water with slices of lemon floating in the ice. He winked at Olivia. Her father's highball was removed by the waiter once all the cubes had melted.

All this time Olivia avoided looking toward the main lobby. Now she examined the horse pinned to her coat. The red ruby-chip eyes looked distended, pop-eyed, too large for the tiny sinews of the long gold horsey face. Olivia unhooked the pin and trotted it across the table. She stood up and trotted it over to the palms and slipped the horse's red eyes through the foliage, pointed in the direction she believed to be her father's. When the horse returned, Olivia asked it what it had seen. But the horse was recalcitrant, and Olivia was forced to see for herself. She pried through the palms. Her father was gone.

The violinist played the opening bars of "Yellow Submarine." Olivia returned to her seat and sat for a moment as if magnetized by the satin stripes of her chair.

She reached into her pocket to check for the twenty dollars her mother had given her for emergencies. There were also several dimes for phone calls and her father's private office number written on a blue index card. In her other pocket she had the messy tangle of bills from her father. She pulled them out and dropped them on top of the table. Although her mother had told her countless times how rude it was to display money, Olivia now arranged the money, not in denominations, but into a little stable for her horse. She leaned the stable walls up against the cream and sugar. She trotted the little horse inside for a nap and dropped the remains of a marshmallow inside, in case he woke up hungry. She stood the boxed panda pin on its side as guard. Still her father didn't return.

Olivia decided to call the office. As she crossed the small auxiliary lobby, the violinist played louder and more insistently as if begging her not to leave. Olivia dropped a dime into the phone and dialed the number written on the card.

Yes, breathed Ann Marie. When Olivia didn't answer, she said, Peter, is that you?

Olivia hung up. It was obvious her father wasn't there. She dropped all the remaining dimes into the phone and dialed her home number. Her mother would know what to do. The phone was silent for a moment, then screeched like a siren in her ear. She must have done something wrong. She put the receiver back so she could try again, and all the dimes disappeared with a jangle. For the first time she began to feel afraid.

Olivia arced back toward the Palm Court. Tea had given way to full-blown cocktails. The band was bouncing, and a woman in silver sang lyric fragments. Olivia checked inside the little money stable; the horse was sleeping. She looked one last time for her father. The violinist edged into "Send in the Clowns," one of Olivia's mother's favorites, and Olivia decided to go home.

Outside the sky was a deep purple over the black trees of Central Park. Several horses fronting carriages stamped and pawed their cold feet. Olivia wondered if it would cost more than twenty dollars to take a carriage to Penn Station and began to approach the first. The artist was stacking up his paintings. He threw one on top of the other and Olivia saw the one she liked tossed face down into the pile.

Someone touched her elbow. She turned to see Nat's solemn face. His goodwill was coming to her as thick and complicated as a honeycomb.

Olivia! Where are you going?

He had the car waiting in front of the fountain.

Home, she said.

Then it occurred to her that Nat was here for a reason. Her father was planning a surprise, and this hiding was part of the game. He was teaching her something. She searched Nat's dark brown eyes. They would tell her the right thing to say.

Are you going to go get my father now? she tried. Nat's face seemed suspended.

Your father said you should wait here until he comes for you, said Nat, but he said it so slowly Olivia knew he was lying.

Did he really say that?

I know he'd be unhappy if you left.

The street had become very quiet. Olivia pushed her hand through her hair and waited for something, maybe for the light to change, for the traffic to start moving. Nat was talking, but she couldn't hear him. She looked up into the sky, the white snow twisted like smoke that went up forever. She put her hands together and laced the fingers. The artist pushed his rusty cart right past her. His face looked frozen solid.

Wait! she said, but the artist kept going, pushing his cart toward Fifth Avenue. Wait! called Olivia and she ran to catch up with him.

I want to buy *Dawning Day,* she reached into her pocket for the twenty dollars her mother had given her. The artist took the bill, rather quickly Olivia thought, then stood there looking at her.

Dawning Day, she said and nodded toward the stack of paintings in the cart.

The artist began to lift the paintings one by one. When he got to hers she cried, There it is! He pulled it from the pile, gave it to Olivia, and then seemed in a hurry to get away.

Nat squinted at the painting, Oh, that's a doozie, all right. He withdrew a white handkerchief from an inside pocket and wiped the surface of the canvas. The odd specks that had attracted Olivia in the first place began to look brighter, as if lit from behind. Just in that moment, her father came spinning out of the Plaza, breathless. When he spotted Olivia beside the fountain he slapped his chest as if she'd thrown something heavy and hit him dead-on. He ran to her and dropped his hands to her cheeks. She could smell him, the clean saddle smell mixed with something sharper.

Don't ever, ever, ever do that again, he said.

Her mother was waiting for her at the train station in Red Bank. Olivia could see the Lincoln parked in almost the same spot; she could see her mother's face glow red as the cigarette lighter made an arc through the dark space behind the windshield. When Olivia reached that end of the station her mother opened the car door. She hopped out and dropped the freshly lit cigarette to the ground.

Olivia felt the sudden burden of all she had failed to bring back with her: the dress, the pins, her father. Her mother found her and wrapped Olivia in her thin arms and kissed the top of

Olivia's head. It was hard letting her mother go. She smelled like a snapped twig, and the wool of her coat was prickly. Olivia pushed her cheek against her mother's lapel.

What's this? said her mother, tapping the painting under Olivia's arm.

It looks like Rome, said Olivia. I bought it myself.

Her mother pulled out a lighter and held the flame toward the canvas to see.

God, if that's Rome, we're in trouble.

Look at the specks, said Olivia. The white parts.

What are those?

I don't know.

Hmm, said her mother. Lights, maybe.

Olivia held her mother's hand until the train left the station, then she let it go and carried her painting to the dark blue car. Inside, she held it carefully on her lap as if the paint were still wet.

Israel

HE BROUGHT VANILLA CANDLES. SOME GIFT. MY MOTHER squeezed them into old silver on the mantle and lit each one. They scorched the wall. Even our best sofas couldn't make up for the cheesy, rundown way the wall looked now. Still, this was London, not New York, and my mother didn't even seem to notice. She was on a date. Derek Duncalf, the anesthesiologist, wrapped his legs down around the last curve of the love seat. My mother bent over, pushed a log back inside the grate. I was saying hello.

Hello, Dr. Duncalf.

My mother said that Derek Duncalf put his patients under by talking to them. But his tedious droning didn't cure him from occasionally leaping across all obstacles to pin my mother to the wall. My mother liked this. She enjoyed the telling of it. She giggled and described his whining and pleading. Their dance of love was set. She would never give in; he would sleep, then spring, then be rebuffed. He sent her flowers: huge sprays, branches hacked from trees in first budding, wired into fanciful shapes. They would lean against the empire mirror in the foyer and my mother would sniff at them, then snore, then laugh.

We were waiting for my father. My father had a small bachelor flat not a block away from us on Upper Brook Street. Every day he would pass by on his way to the office, on his way home. Sometimes he would stop in for a drink. All his things were still with us, half-packed in bags, a favorite painting taken down from the wall, rehung, taken down. Six months of this, eight months, nine months. My mother began to date. My mother began to wear falls—hair attached from the crown of her head that ran down the length of her spine. She loved to wear hot pants and silk shirts and lace-up boots and false eyelashes and brown lipstick and no bra. And though I could see only her faults, the thickness of her upper arms, the glazed look in her encumbered eyes, men came regularly to her living room.

One day Derek brought a friend, Dr. Dan Ovita. Dr. Ovita was from Israel. My mother made a huge fire in the marble fireplace. The flames tossed wild shadows on the silver of her caftan. My mother tossed her fall from right to left, and Dr. Dan Ovita studied her and me. He studied us both, and his gaze made us forget to look out the window at half past six to determine whether my father would be coming for cocktails that day. As it happened, he didn't; not that day, not the next.

Dr. Dan Ovita talked about the war in Israel. The war was fresh. The soldiers were young men and women not much older than me. They were fighting to keep their homeland. Dr. Dan Ovita was the most famous hand surgeon in Israel. He told us that hands were more fragile than butterflies, and when he was able to fix a mortified palm, it seemed a miracle, even to him.

I couldn't forget what he said about hands. My own hands were being leeched of their delicacy by the stones I was gaining. Stones. In London we weighed ourselves in stones—pounds were for money. No amount of dieting, or diet aids, or worse things—abrading my own throat—could help me. It didn't matter. I was getting bigger by the day. My breasts bloomed. But I saw them as two folds among many. By the time my father had been in his bachelor flat a full nine months, I was heavier by seven and a half stones, fifty-four pounds, a pound and a half for every week he had deserted us.

My mother explained: my father needed to forget. We reminded him of all the things he could no longer stand to think of. Without us to remind him, those bad memories shrank and disappeared. He forgot my baby brother's death; he forgot the false indictment and jail; he forgot betrayals and infidelities. He forgot the woman who wrote to my mother saying she'd kill herself, then did, falling from a second-story window. Not so far to fall, but still, she died. Without us, my father was beginning life all over again. He was brand-new, my mother said. He still missed us as people, though, and that's why he visited without calling first, as if he still lived with us. He used his own key, he showered and changed, he smoked and made phone calls. Each time, after he left, my mother found reason to hit me. Once she punched my right breast, and the sensation in that nipple flew away for good.

Dr. Dan Ovita told me that sometimes the men's and women's hands he operated on blossomed like flowers. They became saturated with feeling. Patients took up painting who'd never noticed the color of anything before. People played piano and guitar and mandolins and their families felt haunted and grateful at the same time. One patient who could neither paint nor fathom a tune made hand shadows on walls move like living things. Dr. Ovita was talking about physical therapy, not magic. There was nothing magical about Dr. Ovita, which is why I liked him. He never disappeared; he never changed shape.

One evening Derek Duncalf and Dr. Ovita drank grappa with my mother. They were celebrating because Dr. Ovita had convinced many surgeon volunteers to go to Israel for three-month rotations. By the end of the week he'd be home setting up field hospitals on the borders. They all nibbled on tiny sandwiches I made of pressed-down brown bread and watercress. Their stomachs were barely lined by such things, and the grappa felled them each like a tree. Derek Duncalf's boneless legs rippled down to the floor and I thought his shoe might catch fire, it was so close to the flames. But Dr. Dan Ovita repositioned Derek's body like a kindly choreographer might before melting himself into a graceful puddle on the carpet. My mother's head flipped to the left, one of her breasts scrubbed against her blouse. Under brown silk the nipple looked gnarly and rough, something to scour a pot. That scared me. I couldn't help but run my tongue over my inner cheeks, though she'd never nursed me. Then I went to bed.

Even I was asleep when my father came the next morning to find his blue tie. But I heard him weeping, as I had so often in my dreams. My father's crying sounded like the most deserted baby's, a howling, choking wail. I found him on the side of the bathtub holding his blue tie. He said he didn't understand. He just didn't understand. I felt afraid to touch him. His mouth looked swollen.

Daddy?

Don't, he said.

The only things I could think to say were old things, good things. More things he couldn't stand us for. Especially me. I remembered everything.

I went to find my mother. The curtains were only half-pulled in the master bedroom. Light slipped in from the courtyard. My mother was still semidressed. Hot pants crinkled, wedged at the tops of her thighs, stockings all snagged. Her fall lay at the foot of the bed like a dead dog. Derek Duncalf was stripped completely and his body had little contour, just flesh and hair and a short stub of a penis I could barely stand to look at. He smelled like smoked salmon. I had to stop breathing when I leaned across him to shake my mother. She sat up and her breasts fell into order, the nipples perfect. My father's sobs from the bathroom pulled her toward him, just as she was, like a sleepwalker.

Her hair sprouted in tufts around her face. She pulled my father's fingers from his eyes. His hands were the best part of him. She held them like eggs, very still between her own. My father's face smoothed to a wet red calmness. My mother called him sweet George over and over, which is not his name, not a name I'd ever heard before. Their foreheads touched—she leaning in from her seat on the bidet, he from the lip of the tub. Their bodies made an imperfect arch. I backed out, feeling nauseous, the nausea my mother might have felt when first carrying me. I passed my own bathroom with the green ivy paper climbing to the ceiling, all the way up and across the ceiling, and I passed on the opportunity to suffer my own hand reaching into my throat. I dressed for school. On the way out I wrote a brief note and stuffed it into the pocket of the folded, sleeping Dr. Ovita. I'm coming with you, I wrote.

And Dr. Ovita agreed. My parents said okay, I could go to school in Israel, learn another language. But school is not a big deal to me. In summers I help pitch tents for the surgeons, and I am never afraid. In winter I come to this kibbutz, where I am famous for my cooking and have a soldier-lover with hands that feel like tiny rabbits hopping all over me while I laugh. My hair is very long. I wear a bra as soft as a blanket. My lover speaks to my breast in Hebrew. His guttural sound will surely raise it from the dead. And when I write my parents, my father signs each reply: Our love.

The Widow of Combarelles

PATTY PROMISED HER OLD FRIEND COREN THAT SHE HAD the very best cure for heartache: the shrewd and pitiless French. Brown empty fields late autumn. The view from her stone veranda. Just pack your bags, Patty said. Bring nothing as a gift or I'll turn you away at the door.

For many years, before Patty left for the Dordogne, she and Coren were neighbors on East Ninetieth Street. Patty with three bedrooms and a full dining room on the courtyard side. Coren, only one bedroom plus den, plus a terrace with clear all-season views over low rooftops to the tallest trees of Central Park. On her terrace, Coren tended tulips in pots in the springtime and, in the fall, packed dense gray lavender into copper urns. Fussy, Patty said to her husband, safely. He repeated nothing and Patty hoped she was a loyal friend.

Loyal, but not by nature, she knew. She'd learned the long hard way her own need for discretion and granted it when she could. Patty's son had been trouble every day of his young life until an interest in other planets saved him. Discovered completely by accident on his way out of a third college—this one in Florida. An observatory built to please a new president perched on an inlet. Erupting, volatile stars viewed up close through the telescope could be seen reflected on ripple waves like tiny lit matches. He took up astronomy, and now lived north of Vancouver.

But the years between his birth and his discovery had been challenging and lonely. Patty sometimes felt the company of friends with advancing, adorable children impossible. But what little Coren knew to ask about a child's progress was so far from the rub of daily life it didn't matter. So Patty sat on Coren's tiny terrace in the warm months and drank coffee, wine, and champagne. She ate chocolate, the best bread, sometimes fish, sometimes cheese. In the winter, things were busy from November until March. Then one morning Patty would call Coren and announce with a laugh that the seasons had changed. They'd put on parkas over robes and slippers and go out again with hot mugs to view the first yellow-green tips nudging out of the potting mix.

Coren rarely asked about Patty's husband Brad in all their years together. It was as if she'd never heard of marital discord, and offering gravlax on bitter crackers, or chutney that scorched the tongue, she didn't much chime to Patty's hints. Coren *liked* Patty's husband. And this complete lack of discernment was so calming, Patty decided, as a joke, to take it as a lesson. She'd stop trying to jar him into her own near constant alarm. She would *appreciate* his buffered concentration. He liked his work, the rest he took as it came. He never suffered much. She could admire that. But when he died, stepping out into traffic, listening on his phone to his secretary—who reported tearfully from the podium at his memorial the final crackle and disconnect— Patty's strongest and strangest prevailing feeling was that he'd gotten off easy.

Their son, Brad Jr., was shattered, quietly. He put his head down all the way to his knees and his shoulders shook like a duck in water shaking hind feathers. A surprising tremble along the navy wool of his father's blazer, his narrow back, nipped like a mannequin's at the waist. Darling, she whispered. Brad, sweetheart, and placed her own shaking hand between his shoulder blades. The cool of his skin seemed to penetrate the wool and seep into her fingers. He was very high, she decided, yes, and these shaking tears were no more than an earnest need to be elsewhere. She gave him five hundred dollars when she put him on the plane, and the promise of some kind of trust when things were settled. She went home to dismantle her life.

It was easier than she ever could have imagined. Coren wasn't useful at all. Patty would collapse nightly into one of her silly Adirondack chairs and over the flicker of netted candles report on the chicanery of auction houses and international realtors and estate attorneys. Coren would nod and pour. Only much later, when the walnut trees planted her very first spring in the Dordogne were finally bearing, did Patty realize what a comfort that had been.

Her helpful new neighbor, a farmer who wished to graze his cows in her meadow, brought two dozen saplings and planted each in a delicate line out to the east of her widow's perch. Three years passed, then his sons came to gather the first harvest, and Patty saw an opportunity. She'd return a kindness and maybe settle a ticking disquiet. Almost a fizzy feeling in her nervous system. She wrote to Coren, Come, my dear friend, this place was made for you. It will cure you.

When she didn't receive an answer she telephoned. But even long distance, Coren could be obtuse, a bit dense. What exactly did Patty wish to cure?

Patty laughed, then said, Look, something's come up.

Are you all right? Is Brad okay?

I can't really talk about it on the telephone.

It was odd to think that Coren grew up in Europe because she got so thoroughly lost on the way to the Dordogne. She was stranded a whole long dull day in Amsterdam, where, she told Patty, she'd actually considered calling her mother. As a surprise. Could Patty believe it? I mean everything was completely different, and still I wanted to find a pay phone—there are none—and call and say, I'm home.

You have a home wherever I am, dear, just try to get here. This was the inflated sentiment Patty used all the time, and it protected her. She'd heard the story of Coren's mother long ago. And it was certainly sad. And Coren had been very young. And the stepmother she gained too fast had been feckless and hurtful. All of that, and then the refrain about a phone booth, the most unfortunate detail about her mother's death. Patty felt it was almost tasteless for Coren to bring it up, even obliquely. But this was Coren trying to seed some kind of emotional ground. This would be the trouble: her husband Phil's desertion—it had finally come to that, Patty heard—would equal her mother's early death. Well, Patty had already decided she owed her. That's what she'd realized watching her neighbor's sons bent and laughing, collecting tiny fallen nuts in her young grove. Also that she did precious little in the way of aid and comfort, and maybe it was time.

But willing and able are sometimes very far apart, Patty understood. This case, she could see immediately, was complicated. She watched through the Plexiglas wall in the tiny airport in Bordeaux as Coren shuffled past a customs officer, only to be waved back, then dragged back by a sleeve. His face amused and regretful. His lips quite red and curled. Patty knew the addled woman in gray would be tossed about between bored officers, perhaps even mocked and imitated. She tapped sharp nails against the glass. She caught his startled attention and smiled. This was the right place for her. She knew the right smiles, could calibrate a swift disarming promise. Such a different world and she may have been happier here all along. She was happy now, catching and holding a quick high strike in the eye of a pretty young man. He waved away the woman in gray and smiled an answer to Patty, a promise neither would remember a moment later.

Patty always liked that easy way of playing with things, of lighting small tips of desire and turning away. Just fun. And her husband had never minded, never much noticed. Here it was more intricate, more competitive! And that left her always assessing, sizing up. The doors slid apart, and Coren reached around for a too-short handle to drag a thin red suitcase. She wore a sheath cut like a muumuu, an embarrassing hand-knit sweater, and a nice pair of boots, as if she'd robbed a chicer, cleverer woman. Their burnished coppery sheen looked out of place with the fade of her dress and skin and hair. First thing, Patty would release some closely held information about grooming in one's fifties. Though actually, now that she thought about it, and she had plenty of time, as Coren seemed to lose her way between the automatic doors and the rope fence—Patty's fresh cut roses drooped in her hand —Coren was ten years younger, at least. Not possible, she thought, What in the world had happened? And then she remembered her mission. Aid and comfort, aid and comfort, nothing more. Coren! she cried out, Thank god.

Patty warned Coren about sleeping too long, but it was little use. Coren poured herself into the guest bed and refused, in a complimentary way, to come down for dinner. Such a perfect bed she couldn't move, though Patty's roasting chicken was in all her dreams, the aroma divine. But at five in the morning, Patty woke to the bang of Coren in the kitchen, smashing against the chair rungs. Let her wander, Patty thought, not unkindly; she knew Coren would be happier for the moment on her own. She'd take her in hand in the morning.

Out the high window a sliver of red warmed the black edge of the hill beyond the walnut trees. Patty listened to the knock of the kettle hitting the stove top, and remembered the sad thickness of this landscape when she'd first arrived, before she'd adjusted, and wondered how Coren would see it. But Coren saw so little. It was the secret of her startling equanimity. Patty pulled the duvet high on her chest to smother a prick of unhappiness. A cat, the old gray mother, sighed and settled at her knees.

Their last sleepover, Patty now remembered, had been a disaster. A brownout in Manhattan, both husbands out of town, they'd watched the undulating city from Coren's terrace. The darkness, the sounds from the streets, frightening, but from their perch of safety, fascinating, too. That's when she'd heard the tale of Coren's mother's death and the part darkness played in the violent end of a young foolish woman. Coren's mother had made her fatal telephone call from a booth with a burnt-out bulb. Surely the first thing a girl learns is to avoid the dark alone. Patty released the thought and let sleep take her over.

Patty had a theory about sad stories, they were best left untold. Or told only once if absolutely necessary, then forgotten. So on the first day, spotting Coren wrapped in a blanket staring out unseeing from the stone veranda, she settled on an agenda of distraction. Not easily done in a place where culture had yet to recover from a war most of the world knew only as a reliable movie plot. But there were country walks to be taken, and morning markets to be shopped; she'd invite friends, foreigners who, like herself, had bought up the crumbling abandoned farmhouses and poured money, like honey, into the restorations.

And lucky for both of them, she'd just received a knotty, mysterious letter from Brad Jr. in Vancouver. Darling, she said, letting the letter flutter from her right hand as she balanced a tray with toast and jam and fresh coffee. Help me sort this out, please! She settled the tray on the stone wall and offered Coren a pretty napkin and one of the small white porcelain plates that pleased her so. Good news? asked Coren.

Of course not. Don't be ridiculous. And they both laughed.

Brad's trust was nothing he could live on, but it broke the spirit to have things too easy when young. Didn't Coren agree?

Well, what does he say?

Here goes: *Dear Mama*—great, so far, said Patty, looking up, smiling—*I don't want to bother you because I know you've had a hard time. The project of the house is more than just old stones. If you could be with Dad, you wouldn't need to be out in a field clearing rocks. Right?*

Good luck with the harvest! Be careful of your back. Walnuts are small, but weight is strange the way it accumulates. Maybe that's more about stars.

Anyway, things are pretty good at the Pilner-Stokes, better than at Kaplan-Kolp. The funding tanked when the newest council convened to "clean-up" fiscal slag. Our salaries were cut 10 percent. Unbelievable. But the universe is a long-term project. Anyway, do you think I could talk to Preston Boll about a bigger payout from the trust? Then I could move out of the cave with hot plate, to a studio with a stove and, you know, a shower. I love the work and wish it would pay more. I don't know. Maybe we're both just looking for signs of Dad in something totally mysterious and out there. Anyway, would you consider an increase? If it's a problem, forget it. But if you say yes, you know I'll repay you.

Your son, Brad

Patty folded the letter back into its blue envelope, lifted her cup, and blew on her hot coffee, took a tentative sip.

Very Brad, said Coren. Always so tender. Just like his father.

You think so?

I do! You know what I was remembering in the airport? The way he used to sit with Jorge in the doorman's booth and play gin rummy on rainy afternoons. Poor sad Jorge, remember? His cheeks would swell and that stood for a smile. I remembered the two of them, Brad, a neat stack of pennies—

Stolen.

And Jorge beaming, if you could call it that. Remember?

Of course. And that was precious when Brad peed into Jorge's Thanksgiving dinner. Remember? said Patty, as she leaned over to spoon jam on a toast point.

Really?

You had to calm Jorge down, he wanted to sue!

Oh, come on.

You come on, Patty smiled. Try this toast.

I'm not so hungry.

Patty sighed, You will be. Let me take charge of you this first day.

May I have some more coffee?

Patty peeled out of her teak armchair, scraped it across the stone.

Wait! Don't bother. I thought there was more right here.

No bother.

Coren sighed, looked out at the long meadow. To the right, walnut trees shivered in a breeze, the slender trunks wrapped in a gauzy fog. It was autumn. Ocher underwrote every other color. There must have been flowers in the pergola; their empty pods still reached toward a shrouded sun. Coren snuggled closer into her blanket. Everywhere at this house, it seemed, the high din of flies twisted nearby. A sour manure smell came and went, then Patty was back with a French press glass coffeepot on another enameled tray. I made a ton! But really you shouldn't be drinking it. Anyway, let's table Brad.

But I'm all for a raise! smiled Coren.

Of course you are. Look at those ugly things. In the middle of the meadow, birds too big for the landscape gathered at the top of an old dead tree and cawed. Patty poured the new coffee to the very brim of Coren's cup. Careful! she said, it's boiling.

In many ways the first week was an enormous success. Guy Theirry the retired Swiss pilot flirted with concentration and poise. Patty swore she saw a flicker of interest after the long walk to the nearest village where an atelier boasted a potter of some talent. Guy explained the firing of a certain local clay that required no glaze. The color bursts from within, and no one can predict its beauty. Coren smiled and didn't catch Patty's eye once. Well done, thought Patty. And then watched Guy's large head bob closer to view the squat sphere balanced so carefully in Coren's hand. See the rings, and here, the tiny jabs of flame? he said, All natural.

On Friday, Guy took Coren to dinner. Patty complained of a small headache and used the time to gather her thoughts and make private phone calls. First to Brad Jr.: She was very sorry but completely strapped. She told him, it was funny, his father had made his first million when he was even younger than Brad was now. Amazing, right? What would they do without him? Brad said he loved her and that he had a terrible cold.

Then she called Preston Boll, a funny man who'd always carried a torch for her. She insisted he visit the Dordogne! What in the world was he waiting for! And then they agreed that Brad's trust was best conserved. Unless, of course—Preston Boll reminded her of the terms—Brad wanted to buy a house. There were some nice bargains right outside Vancouver.

Oh, she said.

I know, said Preston, I know. And she could hear the smile in his voice as he said, Just like his old man, head in the clouds.

The stars! And you listen to me, old man, not another peep until you're calling to say you're on your way.

Lonely?

Yes, she said. And she put down the phone. She made a toddy and snuggled under the covers and dropped off before she could even find her book. Again, Patty was awakened in the dark by the bang of the kettle, but this time laughter floated up the curved walnut staircase. The wood was slick from decades of bees wax rubbed into the planks and if she went down in bare feet she might slip. She hunted around for her slippers with the grippy soles and then realized she'd look like someone's grandmother tottering down to scold about the rules. And what rules? A woman deserted by a useless husband making tea for a man puffed with vanity about an ordinary career. Though handsome, Guy Theirry was a complete miss as far as Patty was concerned. No fire. Where the hell were her slippers anyway? Could Coren have borrowed them without asking?

She got down on her hands and knees and lifted the dust ruffle. Here, through the floorboards, directly beneath her, it would seem, she thought she heard the first awkward gasping cry, deep and stupid, as if sounded right in her own ear. Not a bit of humor or grace, a response to what must have been a quick sure grasp on the part of the great pilot. She would certainly not listen to this. Her efforts to rise silently only gave her back a wrenching pull. She would laugh, if it were funny. Here she was, injured by someone else's foolish clutch in the dark.

When Coren finally made her appearance the next day, Patty was out clipping the more artless tendrils of the autumn roses, ignoring the twinge in her back. Patty braced herself for gloating. Dropped the clippers and did her duty: Good Morning, princess!

Oh! said Coren, I didn't see you. Her hand flapped around her heart and she seemed to be panting.

What's wrong?

Nothing, nothing. I was startled. I thought I saw a ghost.

Well, there is one, said Patty, with a smile. She'd landed on the day's activity just like that. We'll have a bite, then walk to the ruins so I can introduce you.

They'd give the great pilot a breather, Patty thought. He was probably home this minute nursing a hangover trying to piece together clues of last night. By the time he called Patty for a hint, they'd be all the way to Combarelles. She'd never liked him, she realized in the moment. Guy Theirry was arrogant. Based on almost nothing as far as Patty could tell. He was tall—true—and had an elegant nose. The rest? His wife died on the operating table and he took early retirement and bought a half-collapsed château for nothing. Every once in a while he gave a course to new pilots.

Patty's first year in the Dordogne, he used to settle beside her at parties and tell amusing stories about young bucks lost in tiny clouds, all very funny. But then no follow up. He was as superficial as the bone button on his fancy bombardier jacket. Oh, she could laugh just to think of him. But why think of him? They'd only been flung together because they'd each lost a spouse in an instant. The macabre things that some people think quicken a pulse. And she could just imagine last night's table talk. Coren would have unfurled some impenetrable tale. And Guy could bore with almost no effort. She wouldn't ask. But Coren was trailing her into the kitchen as though lost. She wore the afghan from the guest room reading chair wrapped around her shoulders and sure enough, Patty's green fluffy slippers. Cold? asked Patty.

Umm, said Coren, settling her back against the wall. She closed her eyes.

He's nice, that Guy, tried Patty, against her better judgement; anything to open Coren's eyes!

Did you know he's found some art under his house? And now there are all sorts of problems with the government. He was clearing the rubble and he actually found one of the women.

The women?

The stone carvings. They're everywhere around here I guess. With the huge bellies? They're pregnant!

Who said?

Well, Guy, of course, and now she blushed. He insists I see them for obvious reasons.

It's obvious you like him! Patty twisted the timer on the convection oven and unwrapped the croissants. I'm just going to give these a little boost. I spoke with Brad last night.

What did he say? I miss him!

So do I. He sounded happy. Loves, *loves* his work. Who ever would have imagined?! I thought he'd be a gangster.

No, you didn't.

Patty smiled, said, Put some clothes on. We'll eat these and then I want to show you something.

But Coren didn't answer.

Patty turned and raised her eyebrows. This was an old cue for them. So many times on Coren's tiny terrace Coren would be choked to silence and Patty would raise her eyebrows. Coren always spilled whatever troubled her. Though what could be so troubling, really, Patty had thought back then. Phil made plenty of money. It was true Coren had wanted children, but it hadn't worked out. Patty assured her it was a blessing. Though the years of trying had been a strain on their friendship. Meanwhile, Phil kept traveling to South America and Coren's terrace plantings became more elaborate.

It was the night of the brownout that Patty heard the baby work was finally over. Coren's uterus was like a clamshell that couldn't be opened and it was all because of her mother. Oh, said Patty, and if only they'd thought to light a candle or two, Coren would have seen the counter cues to the raised eyebrow: the down-turned mouth, the glazed eye. But in the dark, with the stench of burning in the air, Coren said her mother was standing in a phone booth in Amsterdam, probably looking in her purse for another coin. She'd forgotten what kind of cake she'd promised to bring home for dinner. She called the house and asked, then was disconnected.

The police said her change purse was still in her hand but her pocketbook was gone, the light in the booth smashed out. The grocer recognized her, though she'd been shot in the face. She always wore the same sweater, with ducks. The same one she'd worn when pregnant the first time. There was no attempt to save that baby, though there might have been. And Coren told Patty how common it was. Patty didn't reply. She remembers that. And still thinks it was best to keep quiet. But what was so common? She couldn't imagine.

This is Peruvian, said Patty, pressing down on the coffee plunger. Smell.

Guy drew me a little map. Do you mind if I just go?

Mind? No, of course not. Why would I mind?

Okay, said Coren and slumped out of the kitchen. Patty noticed she had an odd smell as she went by. Like leaf litter, wet and acidic; what was it? A mild wafting scent and then it was gone. Patty smiled until Coren rounded the stair, then put the coffee on a tray. Pried the croissants off the oven rack and wrapped them in a paisley napkin. She'd sit herself on the veranda and take a break from her roses. If Coren wanted to join her, fine. If not, fine. She'd forgotten that Coren was a four-year-old. She'd completely forgotten the moods. The dramas. All unspoken, all in pantomime, and the larger for it. Patty lifted the tray, expertly balanced, and opened the side door. Aid and comfort, she reminded herself, aid and comfort.

Her neighbor's sons were drying the walnuts on the stone floor of the veranda, every day the carpet of nuts expanded. She'd kill herself if she wasn't careful. She nudged a group aside and set the tray down on the stone wall. She was dusting new fallen leaves off her chair when the front-gate bell chimed and Guy Theirry appeared in the courtyard with a motley bouquet.

Look at you, how thoughtful! she said and put out her hand. And smiled to see the pilot adjust his strategy and offer it up, the ragweed and juniper, an oily ribbon plucked from some old uniform. Artful, she thought, very good. Have some coffee, just made this very second, she said.

I think, he started, then, yes, of course.

She dusted the other seat. Sit, please, then she moved to sit herself. A little swivel between the chairs. She concentrated on the pouring. Her hands always spoke for themselves. Long fingered, sensuous. She didn't caress the croissants, just plucked one and dropped it on one of her pretty plates. She felt the ease of doing what she was good at, pulled her cup to her mouth and waited, and the pause before the sip brought his eyes there. He grabbed for his own cup and looked out to the old tree in the distance.

You should take that down, he said.

What for?

It's dead.

She looked at him now, at his profile, which was not his best angle. The steep flat forehead matched by a steep flat nose. Black brows, tufted, hectic, above gray eyes. He was squinting, which was his habit, and she started to speak but was reminded, for no reason, of the smell, the leaf litter smell, and an odd conversation she'd once had with Coren's husband Phil on the cluttered New York terrace. Something had died and Phil was trying to wedge it out of a pot. Coren will do it, she told him, puzzled.

She won't, he said. That's just the thing, she lets stuff just sit here. Patty had never noticed. Really?

Then you have no sense of smell, said Phil, whose own handsome nose looked pinched. And that pinch told the whole story. Patty tried to warn Coren. She thought of that period as a kind of negotiation. When Coren remained committed to acting oblivious that period ended. Phil was not a good lover. He was hasty and awkward and paid too much attention to Patty's toes. Things ended quickly and dispersed into the atmosphere like dew.

Outside the gate, the rough engine of an ATV sounded on the gravel. Patty's housekeeper arriving. Grand Central Station, laughed Patty. But the great pilot only frowned. The crows set up a racket, a heavy flapping of wings in the dead tree before lifting off.

It's Marie-Noelle, they're afraid of her! I think when I'm not here she throws poisoned mice under the tree.

And you let her?

Patty gave him a smile. I'll let you forbid her.

Marie-Noelle held open the gate for her mother who carried a new mop. Madame! she cried, pardon.

Please, Marie-Noelle, come, she nodded. They unlatched the front-end door and slipped inside.

Constant companions, said Patty to Guy, watching him, his flat gray eyes; and he watched her, not a flair of interest. He was very disciplined! She'd forgotten.

What should I do with that tree?

Whatever you like, Guy squinted through the kitchen window now, Coren was a vague shifting shape behind the mullions.

Guy pushed out his chair.

Oh, good, yes, you give her a hand. And then Patty caught the scent on his clothes, that leafy smell. Maybe they'd had a romp in the walnut grove, mulch and manure for bedding. They deserved each other. Lifeless rot, both of them. And she astonished herself with the thought.

She was finishing her coffee, taking her time, trying to skirt a rising jitteriness when Marie-Noelle appeared on the veranda holding Patty's green grippy slippers, sopping wet. Madame. In the toilet.

The toilet? Well. The toilet! Really? Patty put down her cup and stood. Maybe we should hang them on the line? Let me see? The toilet, good lord. She almost felt like laughing.

Wait, she bent to brush the crumbs from her new black jeans and a tiny breeze threaded the air. The last of her roses shivered and released a powdery fragrance and she was suffused with ease, just like that. Maybe it was Guy's basic dullness, maybe she'd settled the fuss with Brad. Maybe Coren's troubles, whatever they were, were so beyond the reach of friendship that Patty felt released of any obligation. She did laugh a little. Poor Madame, she whispered to Marie-Noelle, tipping her chin toward the guest quarters.

Marie-Noelle shook her head, murmured that her mother took this as the worst possible sign. The blood.

Blood?

Here, Madame.

Patty could now see the speckles of blood, just on the right foot. She must have stubbed her toe, said Patty, in the dark, in the kitchen. It's nothing, Marie-Noelle. And she nearly smiled, felt grateful to Marie-Noelle and her mother, as she had from the start, for their tragic sense of everything, it relieved her of the burden.

She spoke to Marie-Noelle in French, in an accent that always amused Marie-Noelle. Patty watched Marie-Noelle's stern face as she hinted at an undisclosed trouble in her houseguest, the plan for general, distant coddling, and the specific remedy, perhaps today, of a visit to the widow of Combarelles. Perfect, yes? she said in English.

No, Madame, no, no. Marie-Noelle struggled to find words that Patty would understand, the slippers dangling in her hands. No!

Patty remembered they'd had this conversation before. How could she forget? She'd nearly fired Marie-Noelle on the spot for insolence. The widow of Combarelles was not a joking matter. Her home not a place for a tourist like Patty to go spit out her stupidity and ignorance.

Patty had just been able to gather her own wits and leave the room. At a dinner party that evening, before an open fire, she told the amusing story of Marie-Noelle's frenzy—with amendments.

She called you a murderer? sighed her hostess. Poor Marie-Noelle. It wasn't the Americans. It was the French themselves. Their own fault. They caused the nasty deed.

Then the hostess burst out laughing. She was Italian and had a beautiful throat she displayed, head tilted upward, as if sharing the joke with a passing spirit.

Yes, poor Marie-Noelle, you must apologize somehow, said the host, poking the enormous fire. Make a gesture. Perhaps a candle at the shrine? Then you must be sure to look chastened when you report back. Though I promise the entire village will know about it already.

Just candles? Patty laughed, toying with her silk collar; she had a pretty throat herself. No sacrifices, right? And she thought she saw appreciation in the smile of her host.

But don't let them catch you, that's the main thing, and just in case they do, make it look like you're going to church. The widow of Combarelles is like a saint.

And she'll calm Marie-Noelle?

The hostess shrugged and bit into a wedge of cheese. Try it, she said, then went to see what was taking so long in the kitchen.

It's more a sad story, really, said Guy. This was maybe the last time the two of them were thrown together. (The widow is not the saint of romance, Patty said when asked what went wrong.)

Well?

He lifted his hands to signal the obvious and said, She was a widow. She lived with her mother, just like Marie-Noelle. They worked the cows and chickens, but the fields they left to go fallow. Too much for them. There were walnuts and potatoes and leeks, that's it. This is nineteen forty-three. Maybe forty-four.

And where are the men? smiled Patty.

Conscripted or killed. The women and children left behind were starving. Even the German soldiers couldn't always find enough to eat. But they were lazy, too. And this posting was easy, out of the way. Not much to do. Of course, many cellars of wine to drink.

This *is* a sad story, Patty said. She lifted pleading eyes to her host, ready for the closing punch line, but he was plucking a loose thread on his red leather ottoman.

They lived beyond the long ravine, far from where the soldiers usually found their rations. She stored food, urns of milk, in a cave dug into limestone in the forest. And those still left in the village knew to crawl at night to the widow's provisions. She kept them alive.

Well, said Patty, she *is* a saint! I have some problems besides Marie-Noelle she might be able to solve! She laughed.

But Guy didn't laugh with her. He said, One enterprising soldier, bored by his drunken friends, followed a girl into the woods, and then lost the idea to rape her.

Patty gave up. She told him everything?

Yes. And he killed her, then the widow and her mother. Horrible.

Yes. The mother immediately. The girl immediately, too. Shot through the skull, each. Very carefully. Thoughtfully almost. But the widow he had crucified in the village square. They hung what was left of her on the cruciform you see—every village here has its own, you've seen them?—they hung her torn-up body on the filigree cross and left it for days. Not even the crows dared to touch her. That's what they say, and still you see them gather when, well what's the idea?

The sleepy host jerked opened his eyes, Oh, when a crime of the soul is perpetrated. Isn't that it? The crows are judge and jury. He stretched his arms above his handsome head. God, the heat of that fire. My love? Are we almost ready? he called out.

Terrible, said Patty. Terrible. She smiled a half smile she hoped showed her sympathetic nature.

When the villagers finally found the courage, they buried her with two stones. Because she was pregnant. It would have to be, right?

Ha, I see. Immaculate conception.

Some guess a young boy hiding in the woods from conscription, there were many, but no one really knows.

Probably the soldier who killed her. He knew all along, cried Patty. He was playing a double game, don't you think?

Guy shrugged his disagreement. I doubt it.

Please, said Patty. No more! Uncle! And the host smiled his approval. Quite right, he said, quite right, no more bloody bodies.

Their hostess reappeared by the fire in a new ivory satin sheath, only two slender straps held it in place. Come, please forgive us, we'll feed you at last.

It was a ridiculous story, but Patty took their advice. What else could she do? If she lost Marie-Noelle, no one else would clean for her. Patty knew how small communities worked. Long ago, when Brad Jr. wandered downstairs just once too often to play cards with the doorman with palsied cheeks, she'd let the building manager know about Jorge's odd clinging behavior toward her very young son. Jorge was let go immediately, without warning. And for years, she'd had to flag her own cabs, as if all the doormen of Madison and Park avenues were on notice. No, she would march straight to the shrine and light her best beeswax candles and leave a handsome gift in the little alms box.

She set out first thing the next morning in the prim overcoat and headscarf her hostess had suggested. She half expected a practical joke, that they'd all jump out with cameras. But as she followed the blazes marking the path, she felt the cool shadowy darkness of the thick tree canopy wouldn't allow for much levity. It was a spooky place and a wonder the path was kept clear; better to let this all grow over and disappear. She spotted the high pile of rubble at the trailhead, and smelled a quick spurting stench and then it was gone. As if some animal had been killed in the instant, in flight.

She pulled the gray mackintosh tighter across her chest. There was a constriction here as if the air had lost its power to circulate. Stone shards, old netting, bits of roof tile, shale, and slate. The morning fog hadn't yet lifted, but a votive flame wobbled in a ceramic bowl on the first collapsed wall of the widow's henhouse. Someone had been here before her. What was she looking at anyway? What was so different from the junk she had to clear from her own field? She tossed her coins on the ground and ran.

Marie-Noelle looked nearly as angry today as during that earlier vexed conversation. Patty led the way to the clothesline and studied the blood flecks on her green grippy slippers with what she hoped was suitable gravity. Yes, I diagnose a stubbed toe.

The trouble is clear, Madame.

And then Patty realized it, too. She's sick! The muumuu, the chills, the pallor. You don't think she's dying, do you?

Madame, said Marie-Noelle, with the forced patience Patty had grown accustomed to, even admired. She's with child. Marie-Noelle's mother was quite concerned and would prepare a special broth. They were leaving now. The young madame was in need of great care.

The young madame? said Patty, confused.

This, said Marie-Noelle, nodding to the slippers, A very dangerous sign.

There was one part of Coren's story Patty never quite understood. Some political aspect to Coren's mother's murder. And why her replacement in the household was considered a comrade of sorts. Her name was Sylvia and she resented the color of Coren's hair, flaxen just like her mother's. Sylvia took to calling Coren little clam, because the child was quiet. So when Coren's womb was said to be a clamshell beyond prying at the fertility clinic, it was as if Sylvia had been a seer of sorts.

Patty remembered all this as the last small lever to launch Phil off into his new adventures below the equator. The clamshell, the longing, the suffocating plants. Who could blame him, really, Patty said to her husband. I'll be amazed if he ever comes home.

But Brad Sr. disagreed, which was unusual. She's a love, he said, then looked up and smiled.

A what?

Trust me, he'll get bored.

You mean at home?

No, wherever he is now. Brad shrugged, smiled, went on with the project in front of him, spread across the sofa and all along the carpet. He seldom brought home work, but they were experimenting with face time. Someone had recommended it.

She's a love? Patty asked, That's a new expression for you.

But Brad wasn't listening. And then, so soon, these planned conversations were over.

Patty fixed a light supper and laid the table in the kitchen and waited for Coren to come tell her all the things she'd been keeping to herself. When Guy knocked on the door, it was already dark. She lit tapers as if keeping a vigil and when he sat down long shadows made gray slashes on his flat cheeks. Marie-Noelle and her mother had offered their best but it was clear Coren needed a hospital. Guy had driven her to Saint Cyprien. She would spend a night or two.

Alone? asked Patty.

No, said Guy, her guardians are with her. I just came to tell you, so you wouldn't worry.

And the baby?

Already fragile; she probably shouldn't have come here.

I see, said Patty.

Guy nodded, watched her.

May I offer you something? Patty said.

I won't stay long. I want to check back.

At first he was very quiet, then said, Coren mentioned you were having some trouble?

Patty served the small salad without speaking. She looked at him, kept her eyes very plain, very open. It's nothing, she said.

He shook his head. Let his hands cup the knobs of his knees, the long forearms taut. She could see a tremble there. But when the chicken was on the platter he said some things about the strange place they'd all come to. As if that was the whole story.

Marie-Noelle had told him about the planned outing to the widow. And Patty listened but wished he would stop. Why talk about that? Why talk about her at all, hadn't they learned a thing? Now the village square where the soldiers hung the entrails had mosaics of bright pink flowers. And bauble shops enticed money from the pockets of tourists. Always French tourists. Few foreigners ventured here. Those who did bought up the deserted houses and stayed, because they were safe. They were out of range.

The widow and the war doesn't apply to us, to our happiness, said Guy, and he had that watchful look again, as if there was a correct answer. So why take her there?

Patty kept quiet. He was accusing her of what? Of wrecking a pregnancy with the suggestion of a walk in the woods?

The houses aren't right for us, either, are they?

Patty knew this, too. No, she said, they aren't. Something was always wrong. And if she thought about it, the list was long. Walnuts lost their bitterness but twisted the belly. Her fragrant roses failed to please an inner palette. Good candles carried into the forest did nothing to offset night terrors. And the men who came to comfort lay down and got up again, restless. Her housekeeper was sad and haunted and resentful. The guest who finally arrived after repeated invitation left without thanks or farewell. Later on she just might push the blankets low, the moonlight a flat square in the high window. His face would be a cloudy shape beside her. But for now she knew to keep still. Let him sip and think as if she were nothing but a vapor, or maybe she would be a flame. His choice.

The Aces

RAYMOND HAD BARELY SLIPPED THROUGH THE DOOR when his wife announced she was pregnant. She said it with tickets to Rome. Let's go back to where it all began, she sang. And he decided—after a dramatic pause, sloughing off his jacket, pretending to want to see a doctor's note—sure, why not. It had been a lot of trouble coming to this point and he could tell Megan was ready for a romantic scrim. Their honeymoon just off the Spanish Steps had been hectic and expensive; Raymond lost his wallet three times! He lived at the American Express. But now, ten years later, those memories were vague, and only the beauty of umbrellas bobbing down the ancient street to Ferragamo remained, for Megan.

Raymond still hadn't quite forgiven her for those baleful glances in the famous glove shop. He'd chosen aubergine lined in cashmere, something vibrant yet cozy, and she'd embarrassed him by thinking the gloves were for her. She'd held out her diamond hand and blushed. A flurry of conversation behind the counter among the old men with yardsticks, then the glances. Awful. They left with no gloves for anyone. Lost gloves, lost wallets, that was the Rome he remembered.

This time Rome had been pleasant with only a sour moment or two. Megan's parents arranged the loan of a handsome apartment. A sweet terrace overlooked broken statuary in the garden of the Barberini palace. Good coffee and excellent fruit just out the door, but even the most fragrant orange peeled by Megan's happy hand couldn't extinguish the mild oppression he felt. Even at forty-five, fatherhood had arrived too soon. He knew there were those among their friends who understood him completely, but they hid their knowledge behind fatuous shouts of joy.

The most joyful of all was Megan. And her delight was distracting. She'd forgotten, for example, to select their seats on the flight home. Now Raymond was stuck with a fidgeting neighbor and a direct view to the toilets and the service niche. Seats bolted into the plane as an afterthought. In better times this area would be a spacious avenue, a place to stretch achy calves and suck on plastic cigarettes. But lately airlines had been expanding capacity. Other passengers had in-seat entertainment packages, but for Raymond only a single screen above the curtain to first class promised respite.

Raymond's eyelids began to quiver. The dry cabin air made his head sore. Still trying in her way, Megan swiveled over to the service niche for something anti-inflammatory. Italian stewardesses slumped against the metal drawers. Drinks and salty snacks already flung around, movie cued, they could relax. Raymond inched a hip into Megan's seat on the aisle, slid away from the jittery man by the window. He craned his head to view the opening graphics of a newsreel. None of the wake-up pyrotechnics this network used on land. And Raymond would know. Occasionally he was invited on air to gloss a cultural mystery and he always chose a tie with the visual impact of a space launch. He refused to be outdone by a title sequence.

Raymond tried to concentrate. But there was Megan, inches away, hand splayed on her lower belly. Her contented smile persisted, Raymond thought *insisted,* until the stewardesses were finally obliged to glance down at the hand and beam their sudden understanding. Oh, heads came together. Apple juice was poured *gratis.* She winked her triumph, her happiness at the special status just begun. Then the plane rumbled in a moment of turbulence, the tiny screen flickered, and Megan made a quick grab for the roll bar above the coffeemaker. She found her footing and beamed. A mime of a brave chin-lift to signal he need not worry, she and the baby were fine.

He pushed the earbuds in tighter and dialed up the volume. Yet another former government authority had made an intemperate comment about the Muslims. Raymond listened to the clip. The man was retired so had no real clout. But the newsreel took his notion seriously enough to illustrate it. Raymond watched as a series of women's faces appeared, all quite pleasant, each unsmiling but ready to smile, ready to listen and give a kind response. It was mildly disturbing. This parade of maternal-looking women. And it seemed to go on forever until finally the last with her veil. Only her eyes showed, dark, registering little emotion, just shapes above a blackened field, and Raymond felt relief. Sudden and powerful. As if he'd been granted an inner stay. He wanted to laugh. Just on this plane, how pleasant it would be if every woman, his wife with her superb joy included, could have the option—just the option!—to bring it all back inside.

What an idea! Men were just better this way. You weren't bombarded with personal feelings at every turn. Even the guy by the window squirmed in squared-off patterns, probably planning a crop rotation, not a romance. It was exhausting. And here was a simple answer, quite popular in some places. What was the big deal? But the voice-over and the retired high-level government official disagreed with Raymond. In a jovial voice, a tone that said this is obvious to us all, the overdub concluded that the veil was problematic. It cut off communication in the wider world community. And the very next thing, Raymond was looking at advertisements for perfume and Scotch, just the items confiscated at duty-free because he was flying to America.

He wished Megan would sit down. At the same time, he edged farther into her seat and closed his eyes. An animated film about the love trials of a racing car was about to begin. Not interested. He turned the earbud volume to buzz. It might be possible to nap. He curled down lower. Megan's seat smelled of baby oil and something even less appealing, like an antibacterial rub. He wondered if they'd ever have sex again. Doze, he told himself. Though sleep often brought such unpleasant ideas.

There'd been plenty of dreams about Helena. But now, closing his eyes, he didn't even need to sleep. He'd had a shock. A close call. Or was it? Raymond wasn't quite sure how to parse it:

They were sitting in a café, in a sticky red booth, under an enlarged photograph of Audrey Hepburn. Megan felt she resembled Audrey Hepburn and kept her hair styled in the duck-tail fashion of the early 1950s. As long as she kept her weight down, this looked okay. But right after the wedding she'd been less watchful than before. You look like a fat little boy! he shouted in their worst fight. The fight that cleared the air and marked the outer limits of aggression. She'd been on a diet ever since. But now, in Rome and pregnant, a daily craving for fettucine alfredo had set in.

So there they were, indulging a yen, when in strolled Helena. Helena on assignment in Rome. Ho ho! he laughed, oh my god! He peeled up and out of the booth. You remember Megan, of course. And Megan stood, too, belly pushed forward. She offered her hand and the victor's smile he'd seen before.

But Helena's face crumpled like a collapsing wall, so vivid in her distress. He forgot she'd never met Megan. Oh! he said, this is my wife, and darling, this is that wonderful young woman I told you all about.

Megan smiled. Helena stayed very still. As if he might forget her, as if she could give him the slip even now. Kind of comic, really, but then he remembered that maybe he'd been a bit of a bastard. Maybe he'd said some things about Helena he shouldn't have. But the whole *Newsweek* mad-girl-stalker story was really not his fault. That was a mistake. A mistake that, by the way, happened years ago, really in another lifetime. And here he was celebrating, sort of, with his wife! A wife Helena had always known about. And there were those funny knees again he liked so much.

Megan kept up the chitchat. So great to meet you! Yes, fabulous place to visit. You live here? Wow. But guess what? They had the best news ever, and so on. Helena looked like she might throw up. Made an implausible excuse, something about Hermes, then waved good-bye. Megan dropped back into the red banquette, gaze fixed on her platter. She mopped up the cream sauce with the last heel of bread and didn't raise her eyes again until she asked with a more open appeal: dolce?

All the tears, all the drama. Not some fateful twine of love and work, as Helena had claimed. Just *hormones,* Megan's favorite word. Or sex, and even now that wasn't entirely out of the question. He'd ask around when they got back to New York. Find out what Helena was up to these days. Meanwhile, on the screen the purple cartoon race car winced and cavorted and Raymond thought about the women in the newsreel. Helena would have a strong opinion about the march of those faces. She wouldn't agree with Raymond or with the government official, but then her opinions were often contradictory.

For example, their very last time together, she was both finished with him and full of urgent offerings. First weeping and wailing, mostly about Kamal and about how he, Raymond, was a monster. Then she admitted she'd barely been alive in some part of herself. Kind of dead, you know? Until I met you.

So Raymond was her prince. Then he was a bastard prince. Then he was just a bastard. He wanted to destroy everything around him. He wanted to ruin the thing that mattered most, her work!

Helena was silly and amusing. He remembered laughing and making a seductive gesture, Let me ruin you now. Something that had always been welcome before, a sweet *come here, you little nothing*. But she was in a childish mood.

It's not funny! she cried. Next she'd be stamping her foot. Those knees trembling in a way he found intriguing, but for the moment she whimpered, And how does it help you? That's the part I really don't get.

He didn't get the question. He'd pushed her through baby steps. Read her pages. Listened to her ideas when courtesy demanded. He'd given her plenty. What was the big problem? But she was on to Kamal again and how Raymond was the one who deserved to be arrested.

Finally all the poor posture and sniffles made one last back-flip into balling. The tweed sofa creaked and crackled. Then he was wriggling out from beneath her sweaty legs, heavy as fallen bricks.

What are you eating? he said, only teasing, he liked the narrow gauge of her. She was all bone, dense heavy bone, and she kept him pinned. Please, she said. *Please,* at least try to get him a decent lawyer?

Oh, come *on,* he said. Surely they were done with Kamal. Who do you think I am?

The first time he saw Helena she had a fistful of new peonies and was haggling for a better price with that cheapskate Lebanese Kamal. He sold burned coffee and buns in a tiny loamy-smelling storefront near Raymond's office in the flower district. They're buds, she said, not even real flowers. Raymond could see this was an old game for the two of them.

Kamal frowned, then smiled, then wiped an imaginary load from his mind and waved her away. Take them, little monster, he said with an exaggerated accent. You fleece me and I like it. What's wrong with me?

Indeed, thought Raymond, who always bought there, and always felt the fleecing went the other way around. The flowers were usually half-wilted. Coffee twice heated on principle. Kamal was a crook, but a convenient crook. No one else in the neighborhood sold retail.

She smiled, Helena smiled, and kept her hand holding the unbloomed flowers quite still. Only her chest raised up a little to place her whole slim frame at a better angle. Very pretty, thought Raymond. And wondered how old she was? Guessing twenty, maybe twenty-one, with a touching case of physical immaturity. But Megan had a dinner party that night, and his job, *his only job,* she liked to point out, was to find some flowers and bring them home. Anything, as long as they're not dead, she'd said.

That evening, as promised, he arrived before the company did. I'll jump in the shower, he told Megan.

Don't splash the floor, she called, I just finished scrubbing. Then she stood on the threshold while the water ran over his hot head. His flower offering gathered in her smallest vase. Oh, Ray, she said, these things aren't even open.

Now the airplane was desert dry. His shoulder pinched against the outside armrest. Megan tapped him right where it hurt the most. He started and looked up at her with some alarm. Ray, she mouthed, hanging her face above his. He pulled the earbud out just an inch to listen.

Don't worry, sweetheart, but my ankles are swelling. The stewardesses found me a seat in first class. Megan lifted an elastic cuff to show the ridge marks deep in her skin.

Fabulous, he said, and leaned down to assemble his belongings.

Just me, she giggled, unless you're having sympathy bloat.

Well, this was preposterous. Megan in sweatpants slipping behind the impassable curtain, the fidgeter sliding halfway into Raymond's seat, a woman he'd virtually handed a career to skittering back wide-eyed from a pleasant encounter as if he were holding an explosive. What was the world coming to?

Of course, Helena hadn't exactly been his assistant, but she was something professional. He let her fill in the blanks now and then. She wasn't good at it, he had to admit, sadly. And she was flaky, disappeared for days at a time. But something was working, maybe just the look of her stretched out on the brown tweed sofa squinting to decipher the nonsense of his rivals. He loved when she tossed things over the back of the cushions or faked a swoon from the noxious fumes, or pretended to puke. He liked how her face actually went purple, then released back to her normal pale. And once she lit something on fire. He thought she was kidding, but sure enough, the smoke alarm went off before she could hustle the thing into the loo and snuff it out.

But everything he wrote, from index cards to e-mail, she read with reverence. She went very still when she had some page of his in hand. And it eased something in him to watch her then, so quiet and concentrated. He found himself believing in her faith in him, and he wondered at his own delightful innocence. There all along. Like some wide silvery sky outside his office window. Sometimes she'd drag out some hidden scrap of her own, minor in every way, but he gave her the amniotic approval she desired. He thought they were happy for a while. Then Helena had something else to show Raymond. A printout of a tiny blip she'd published on the Internet. Right away he could see there were problems.

Wow, he said.

You think?

Uh, yeah.

Really? She beamed at him. She was gorgeous in a new way. But her teeth looked unpleasant. He preferred her old smile. And her eyes were weird, like there was nothing stopping them. Bottomless open-ended interest. He had a responsibility here.

Okay, said Raymond, what's with all the death?

The death? she asked.

The brother *and* the mother? Incurable childhood cancer *and* a car crash? I mean, it's only three pages long.

Um. It's an elegy? I know the rule for fiction, but essays, it's okay to just say what happened. Right?

He shook his head. Pick one. Probably the mother because vehicular manslaughter is more interesting. Then: light touch. Just itsy-bitsy teeny-weeny hints.

Her smile went very wide and stuck. Is this a joke? she said.

Joke? he said, then suddenly realized he was supposed to go home early. I'll be right back, he said. Next time, show me first! He waved, then flew out the door.

Waiting for the elevator he wondered if she'd become distracted now. Get herself tangled up in old griefs. Start messing things up. Of course, he'd had tough times himself. He hated to think about all that. But now she'd triggered a bleak image: Friendly's. His parents, each in their own separate sport vehicles, arriving on alternate weekends at school to take him to brunch. The really great thing about Megan? She'd never even lost a tooth. She had only happy, healthy relatives and tonight they were coming for dinner. He stopped by Kamal's for his cheapest bouquet.

Where's the little princess? Kamal asked.

Working, said Raymond, digging in his pocket for some coins.

You don't think so?

Of course I think so. What's it to you?

She's a good girl. You know, she lives here a long time, right there, Kamal nodded toward some blue scaffolding. Since she was a little child. I know the whole family, from before, you know. The mother was a kind woman, still no one can believe what happened, if you hear me. Kamal waited, then handed Raymond the cone of flowers. The girl tries very hard for you, that's what I'm saying, makes sacrifices.

These are the ugliest flowers you've ever sold me.

No, sir, Kamal laughed with what sounded like admiration. For you, I have much worse, believe me.

Raymond laughed, too. The flowers stank like something scooped out of a compost heap. But Megan knew how to deal with bouquets. She had tricks and remedies.

*   *   *

The next day Helena's little things—her personal stapler, her emergency cardigan, her bluish lip gloss—were gone. And Raymond got the message and was surprised how painless it was. Freeing, he told himself. But a few weeks later he saw her tucked inside Kamal's little storefront between the tinned biscuits and the Miracle-Gro. She was talking so softly he only overheard a single word: irreplaceable. Then Helena looked up with a radiant expression. Worshipful, in fact. And he felt himself drifting toward her, entranced as well, until Kamal poked him hard in the ribs. Out, please, sir. Nothing for you here today.

Even from the sidewalk, her face seemed to say: There's no one and nothing I'd rather see than you. And he thought, it's true, there's no replacing that. Then Kamal was shoving and stepping on his good shoes. Blowing sour disapproving breath all over the place. Watch it, bud, Raymond said, and Kamal said, Just let her be, please. I'm begging now.

But an hour later, there she was, back on his brown tweed sofa. Tiptoed in and picked up some folders like nothing had ever happened.

I have news, she said.

Can't it wait? he asked, fingering the pretty ridge of her hip bone.

Not for very long.

Thinking back, he'd misunderstood her meaning. He assumed she meant: Let's fool around and then I'll hint, urgently, at some feeling best kept under wraps. But it turned out she was talking about something else. During their period of estrangement, Helena had gained a minor victory. A new journal, *Heron's Flap Quarterly,* was about to publish a personal essay documenting her apprenticeship to Raymond. Apprenticeship? Had he agreed to this? Maybe it was better he hadn't? Sometimes, he believed, Helena exaggerated his goodness.

But no sooner had the honor dawned then a hand-painted sandwich board appeared outside Kamal's shopfront accosting all pedestrians. A deceptively prim head shot of Helena wearing a turtleneck and a schoolgirl smile was laminated to both sides. She smirked at all comers. Many paused to consider her expression, then shelled out good money for galleys xeroxed on wax paper wrapped around a bunch of rotting rosebuds. Twenty pages detailing Raymond's career philosophy. The title? *Dead-head: Every Bud a Weed to Crush and Kill Me.*

Raymond spoke to Kamal, man to man. Reminded him of their long fruitful association. But Kamal said, It's a free country! The little girl can speak her mind.

Raymond tried once more. He told Kamal about Helena's *problems.* He made a circling gesture in the crotch region to indicate something fairly horrible.

Kamal refused to listen. Out, he said. Don't come back, please.

On the sidewalk Kamal straightened the sandwich board so Helena's malevolent mug dared him to say another word. And

Raymond was forced to do the only responsible thing, should have done it ages ago. He called the number posted pretty much everywhere and reported the funny looking people drinking poisonous coffee in the shadows of Kamal's establishment.

When he phoned the *Heron's Flap Quarterly,* they were delirious just to hear the sound of his voice. So modest, they said, so unassuming. They'd take care of it immediately. A much better experience than the dysfunctional anonymous city hotline.

And that was the end. Helena came to his office the one final time. The day of all the contradictory weeping. He thought only colicky babies could cry so hard. No one knew where Kamal was being kept!

Kept? Raymond said. He's traveling! Maybe he's gone home to Beirut. Raymond shook his head. Don't worry. You worry too much. And it will only get in your way.

Soon the flowers died in earnest in the little storefront. A latch and padlock were installed. Strips of yellow police tape crisscrossed the door. The sandwich board was tossed inside, but if he pressed his face to the window at dusk he could see Helena's picture, just the eyes smiling and the letters "Crush" in a Gothic script like a love note she'd left behind.

Just thinking about her made his nostrils sting. His toes and fingers went numb, his inner ears itched, and his eyelids swelled. Some cheap toxic economy-class cleaning fluids emitted nearly visible waves that would probably blind him. And

Megan was no doubt off getting a foot massage from the stewardesses. It seemed just yesterday when the good news she hurried to deliver was that she'd finagled a way to upgrade *him. He* needed rest, he needed to be on top of things. She used to take pleasure in making things go well. But six weeks of pregnancy and she was hustling for herself alone. Raymond shook his head but that only increased the vertigo. And if he had to sit one more minute with the fidgeting guy, he'd shoot someone.

Though of course he didn't have a gun. He didn't even own a gun, didn't believe in them. Once, after Friendly's, his father had taken him hunting near his boarding school. It was all winter white out in the woods. Raymond was on magic mushrooms like nearly everyone in his senior class all that last semester. When his father made a direct hit to the doe's abdomen and the blood spattered so red on the snow, Raymond burst into tears and could only be soothed by a priest in the local Catholic church. Up until then, Raymond's family didn't even know any Catholics. But now his father had to buy a pew. And he still hadn't quite forgiven Raymond. At least that's what Raymond always says when he tells the story: This is how a boy becomes a man in America. And he always gets a laugh of recognition, of understanding. Except, of course, from Helena, who had fairly insane ideas about priests—she was raised by Vatican II zealots—and deer, she thought deer were endangered. Look, he'd told her, it's a story about me, forget the priest, forget the fucking deer.

But Helena was unconvinced. Again. She heard the hunting trip as a story of sexual enticement and animal torture. The priest had only cradled his head, Raymond insisted. His father was in the room the entire time. Helena could believe what she wanted. What she believed, apparently, was that he was turned on by dead deer and old head-holding priests. No, no, no, he'd told her, he was high on *mushrooms.*

Thinking back on that conversation, he understood that if it hadn't been for her face, none of it would have mattered. If he hadn't seen that look of hers, he wouldn't care if she couldn't understand a simple story he'd told a dozen times before, in front of audiences who got it completely and applauded. Sometimes on their feet, sometimes with tears in their eyes. Most exuberantly of all at the alumni reunion of his boarding school. But he always waved away the adulation, didn't he? He'd say, No, no, come on, now, his irony and self-effacement completely apparent. Helena was blind. And her face, that come-hither-no-prisoners face of hers was distorted by a vision only she could see.

He hoped. He hoped only she could see it. And though he was fairly certain that was true, he started dropping little hints about her credibility to open ears here and there. In a precautionary way. And it was gratifying how quickly the innuendos, the half thoughts took on a life of their own.

Now and then people still asked, What ever happened to her? He heard she was sick for a while. But now she'd pitched up in Rome of all places, looking healthy, except for all the skittering back. What to make of that? He tried to recapture her expression just as she left the café. She wasn't laughing, was she? Probably crying. Whatever she was doing, he realized, he *finally* realized, it was making him kind of furious.

Yes, they'd had talks about men and women, and deer and priests, some of them good, some of them ludicrous. But the chief thing to understand about Helena was that she was enraging. He felt that rage pumping in a pleasant, familiar, enlivening way across his chest, opening up his sinuses. He felt sharp and alert for the first time in forever and blinked open his eyes to see the least attractive stewardess charging down the aisle right for him. Now the fidgeter was bouncing in his seat, swatting at the back of his pants.

Good Christ, said Raymond.

The stewardess leaned into their space and the guy shouted, There are fleas in my seat!

Now, sir, calm yourself, she said. And Raymond sat far back and closed his eyes. Raymond was afraid of fleas. Nothing he could do about it. As his neighbor climbed over him, all outerwear and wriggle, Raymond clamped his mouth shut and commanded himself not to scream. No screaming. No screaming, it was his own kind of mantra, and he'd discovered it worked in a variety of situations. And now it was helping already.

The stewardess hustled the man to the restroom while Raymond quickly determined, from certain clues, that the problem was all in the guy's head. One, nothing leaped up and down in the window seat. And two, wouldn't he, who was so susceptible, be the first one bitten? Without moving his head, he kept a tight surveillance on the mash of nuts and pretzels.

The one truth he'd actually been able to teach Helena, very early on, when she first came to work for him, before all the trouble began and she became such a deep and incurable pest, was this: Stone hard, unrelenting confrontation rewards itself.

What do you mean? she'd said, that gentle, open face not fooling him for an instant.

People call you a louse and a pretender, just stare them down until they evaporate.

Raymond?

That's right.

Raymond, *no one* thinks you're a pretender. Sometimes, it's a little nutty in there. She pressed a small finger to his temple. Then she was tossing aside the throw pillow and standing up. The rough tweed of the sofa had left red imprints along the tops of her thighs like he'd branded her. See what I did? he said, rubbing his fist across her skin.

I'm dehydrated, she said, twisting to look, frowning down. She slumped into the bathroom and slammed the door. A second later the sink started pounding. He listened, then thought, *What?*

Hey! he was up and shouting through the locked door, What do you mean, *No one thinks I'm a pretender?* Who have you been talking to?

The water boomed away until finally she was back in the room wearing a stretchy black miniskirt and a lavender blouse with torn ruffles. There were big water splotches down her front. Her shampoo smelled like burning asbestos.

Answer me. What have you been saying about me?

She rubbed his only hand towel in her wet hair. Her eyes took on an expression best used for viewing newborn kittens. That you're beautiful, she smiled.

I'm serious. Who, what, and where, right now, tell me.

Raymond, don't be silly, I adore you! She dropped the towel on the floor and sat next to him on the edge of the sofa. She wore the prim smile that would soon gross out the neighborhood from a sandwich board.

He wouldn't look at her, she didn't deserve that kind of courtesy. But then again, why not stare her down? Who the hell was she?

Raymond? Raymond. Everyone I know thinks you're *amazing.* I've been in awe of you since the day I was born. Before, in fact! My mom used to listen to *Why Me?* on tape when I was in utero! And when I was little? She read me the sad childhood parts of *Only Genius.* How the low IQs of your siblings isolated you? In my case, it was, you know, an actual death. So the IQ part wasn't as pressing. But the loneliness was the same. And I could get through somehow, just because of you and your essays. The worst, most impossible things became bearable. Kind of.

She seemed compelled to display those impossible things now. Curling her mouth, filling up her eyes with chaos. I know you understand because you understand everything. Just try, just a little, please?

Try? He should *try*? Fuck her. He bolted off the sofa and commandeered the bathroom. Flooded as usual. He waited, seated on the lip of the tub, feet on the toilet, eye on the lock, for her next move. It was a long wait. Then he heard the quiet click of the front door closing. A bad sound by any reckoning. And next thing his head was in his hands and he felt like crying. He'd been working too hard. And now some dopey chit was out testing the market on his success. Telling him horror stories to boot. Megan never messed with him in this way. He let out a shuddering sigh, he couldn't possibly detest Helena more. But then she did something even worse. She came back. Three light taps on the hollow door, Hey! I got us some coffee. Please, come out. I'm an idiot.

No news there. But he'd withstood a lot more than some baby succubus in a wet blouse.

Raymond? If the way I feel about you? If that's the problem? Don't worry. I get it completely now. I said something stupid about love?

Oh, boy. She seemed to be speaking from the floor. He could see the shadow of her head moving on the threshold beneath the door. The little pink spot of her lips pressing in. And now he noticed the tiles around the sink were coming loose, she was wrecking everything.

Raymond, she whispered, please. This is killing me.

He was nearly seated in the aisle when Megan returned from her stolen nirvana with a peace offering. He could tell by the unfocused smile. Wow, he said, squinting. I can barely see.

It's that bad?

Yup.

Come on, you, she said.

Come on, what?

She pitched her head back with a playful wink. With her Audrey Hepburn haircut growing out, sideburns were curling in front of her ears. He followed her glance and saw her friends the stewardesses had sequestered themselves behind a drawn metal door to prepare dinner. Follow me, she said.

He gave her a look to say his indulgence had a short lease. This better not be about herbal tea. But no, she was leading Raymond behind the magic curtain and tucking him into the very last seat in first class. She'd made a sweet little nest, with M&M's and Scotch on the rocks, his personal weapons against every trouble, large and small. There was even a flower in a tiny stick-on vase. For me? he mouthed.

Who else? she whispered. She blew a kiss then tiptoed back out to economy. And he understood. All the bloating, all the coyness had been a ploy, an act, she was still his ace in the hole. And he was hers, of course. He settled deep into the leather ergonomic recliner, a perfect fit! He pressed the release until he lay nearly flat. Every muscle in his body relaxed into the cushions. He turned his face toward the closed window shade, the rising sun completely obscured. It was peaceful here and Helena was far away.

Farther away by the second, back in Rome where he wouldn't return for a very long time. And when he did, he'd be a father. Something Helena would never understand. How could she? He was safe. A whole new time well begun. He pulled the sleep mask over his eyes and a smoky lavender scent whacked him into a lulling contentment. There were hard truths out there just waiting to be dusted off. And he would do it.

May Day

FULL CHOP IN THE WATER ON FRIDAY EVENING DIDN'T necessarily mean no sailing in the morning. All week, her husband had fulfilled the list of tasks he'd written down on a yellow legal pad as if he'd never done them before. Then the enormous worry about time. And what about the new owners at the marina, could they be trusted to get the basics right, get the slips ready and the buoys secured, mark the channel, clear the fallen trees from winter storms, clear out the boats of the dead? Sad truth, they were an old dwindling club and every spring brought a tag sale of leather cushions and rusted saucepans. The old boat dragged to inland children wherever they were. Once, Philip Kellstone drove to Oregon with a Chris-Craft twenty-footer. My great adventure, he called it. The new marina owners were unlikely to keep up the tradition. Already they were making noises about a dance club overlooking the inlet, and family memberships for a swimming beach. Who in their right mind would swim in the Hudson? But they claimed the cleanup would be better than anyone could imagine. They'd import pink Bermuda sand. And sell organic fruit drinks.

He was thinking of a change, he told his wife. The decision to stay or go wouldn't affect her, it was purely his thing, but he looked so forlorn.

They were standing in the upper parking lot of the Rhinecliff train station, getting the full vista of the whitecaps on the water and the gusts in the distant trees, a lowering gray in the sky. So unlike Mother's Day last year when every flower in the Hudson Valley had bloomed right on time, but Melody hadn't come, and hadn't for a very long while. This year the forsythias were still green and nearly closed, only sparse tips of yellow. The lilacs were just budded, no more, and wisteria hung with desiccated fronds. Wouldn't you know it, said his wife.

She doesn't bother with that kind of thing anyway, he said.

Oh, I don't know, I always thought the garden mattered in a way, maybe not so much to talk about, she said.

She says what's on her mind. No big mysteries there. I promise you.

His wife kept quiet, and opened her eyes wider toward the river. She shifted her hand above them, but there was little sunlight to block out. Her eyes felt strained, nearly distended in their sockets, as if she had extra-duty seeing to attend to. She felt serious, settled, grounded in new ways, tried, You'll be fine tomorrow. This breeze is just stirring the pot out there.

He nodded, and the train blew a sharp hoot coming into the station. She caught a first sweet gush of a lilac scent out of nowhere. He started down the stone steps to the station. She smoothed the front of her skirt and followed, looking carefully as she went, holding tight to the rail.

The train was on time. And crowded. So many people taking the large leap from the dangling silver platform in the train door to the three-legged plastic stool like a toddler's plaything. Too big a step, she thought, for some, and felt no impatience when the conductor slowed someone down, let the bags be passed into his arms first before a tentative foot was allowed. Sixty, maybe seventy, people got off the train, but who would have guessed that Melody would travel all the way in the very back, the car barely in the station.

She spotted Melody first—over there!—yanking a green rolling bag off-kilter, something out of whack with the wheels. There! she said, and started the zigzag through the Friday commuters too tired to let her by. She lifted an arm and waved but nothing too flashy, she didn't want to embarrass Melody, as she knew she'd done in the past. She wasn't too old to learn how to get along with the people she loved. No one was. Melody, she said, low, smiling, and only the old conductor caught her voice and smiled back. He'd been around forever, and held his arm out stiff for the young mother making the jump out of the train. Melody, she said to herself, felt the draft of her husband behind her. Excuse us, he said, please. They were moving in entirely the wrong direction.

The daughter looked up, saw the mother's face, stopped moving, and dropped the ragged strap on her bag and rubbed her shoulder, until they were close, then said, Hey, Daphne, hi.

And the mother frowned but caught herself, reminded herself of she wasn't sure what. There was no time for analysis, except whatever Melody wanted to call her that was okay, wasn't it? Sweetheart, she said back, and she reached out and felt, quick as a leaf brush, the dry tired peck from her tall, too-thin girl. Long trip? she asked. Though she knew the timing to the second. Are you tired?

Nope, said the daughter, who looked, at thirty-five, not a great deal different than at nineteen, too thin, dark sad circles under her eyes, a halo of black hair all in squiggles near her shoulders. What now, the mother thought. But she felt her eyes relax, the commuters jostled her in their hurry, she didn't mind. The same thrill rushed through her, and wasn't it silly. This girl-woman who barely spoke to her, wouldn't call her Mother, because she didn't deserve the title, that's what Melody had said at nineteen and apparently stayed with the decision, this teetering frowning wretch could fill her with such happiness. It was ridiculous, and so certainly chemical. A great rise and something she should discuss later on. Sweetheart, she said again, thank you. Thank you for coming.

Her husband picked up the green suitcase, said, Hope you brought your sneakers! Boat's in the water.

You think I'd miss it? asked the girl, who looked committed to missing everything.

Not in a million, he said, hefting the suitcase higher, showing off. The train already just a dark distant groan. After you, he smiled, following slowly, struggling now to settle the unbalanced thing against his chest while the mother waited below to watch, perfect, as Melody climbed the whole long way up the high stairway, so quick and light and lovely.

Guidance

IT'S NOT LIKE I GAVE UP A LOT IN LEAVING TOKYO, BUT
I did forgo a few things I barely knew I counted on. My roommate, for instance, and our apartment in the Roppongi district.
The tatami mat bedroom and the electric rice cooker. Who
knew that rice was slimming? We were models, and then, so
quickly, I was married. My husband three times my age, but
handsome. Tall in the American fashion, his chest lifted up and
wide. Not like the drooping tulip boys we left behind, not like
old Stefan and Hec. Better to be thick-topped, compact, than
bent over and complaining about a bad back every second of
the day. Or debating the taste of vinegar and fish, good, bad.
All of that is no longer relevant. And my roommate, Betsy,
might have to find her own American husband now without
my help.

At first Betsy was welcome at all my new husband's parties.
Then, one morning after an impromptu sleepover she may have
made an unsavory observation, maybe a sarcastic remark about

an important friend or client. Not that I was paying attention, I don't even know where she slept! But next thing I knew, my husband was saying, Out! And hustling her toward the foyer. She barely had time to find and grab her model's bag, a satchel full of every secret to keep us beautiful. She tracked all of that, and once she was gone, I had to learn to improvise. I'm still not even twenty, so I have options. But I miss her.

Betsy wouldn't much like it in Jakarta, it's hot. But there were compensations. I had my own compound, for instance, built of stone with marble floors even in the garage. The servants had a small wooden hut, without any floors, so it was very easy to tell who was who. I suspect this was where Betsy ran into trouble with my husband, saying whatever she thought to everyone. There was privacy in Jakarta, not that I was looking for that, I had no problem sharing a tatami with Betsy. At the compound I had a master's suite, a dressing room, and a terrace where I could sit naked because no one could possibly scale the twenty-foot wall, and since the air space was embargoed small planes and helicopters were out of the question.

I did get a quick thrill one day early on when a young servant, Mustache, ran through my private terrace with a machete. He was chasing the ratsies he said and held his hands wide so I understood the pressing nature of the hunt. Mustache seemed not to notice my breasts or the unusual pattern of my pubic hair—I liked to change it pretty frequently, but not as often as

Betsy!—he seemed blind to me, except to the notion of a superior being who required an explanation. He trembled not with lust—I really know the difference—but with fear.

You're okay, I said, but that wasn't enough. Okay! I barked, adding a haughty growl. He bowed his head, so like Stefan and Hec, though small and malnourished and brown-skinned. Okay! I said again, and he backed away. And I rested on my chaise. I put my ice water to my forehead. I had a nice little fantasy about the urgent reason for his surprising appearance, and poof, I came, with barely a tickle. A heat situation, I wanted to tell Betsy all about it, as if she might move after all for the crazy advantage. But it wouldn't last. Soon I was pregnant with twins, and an entire squad of Mustaches with machetes would leave me supine and quiescent. Big words. I'm starting to read my way out of here.

I like to think I made an impression on Dewi Sukarno and that's why I came to Jakarta at all. It happened right when Betsy became unmentionable. That morning, after showing Betsy the door, my husband waved my life management book before my eyes like a magician, slow backs and forths as if I wouldn't catch on right away. Then he walked to the balcony rail and with an overhand toss released it to destiny. There was a whole career in that book. I hoped some beautiful girl from Denmark with a knack for clearing her face of all expression, letting the textures and colors speak the human language, someone just like me, might pick it up and continue where I left off. Like a torch passing, because I'd done some very jazzy work already.

But there was Dewi, in an off-white silk suit, her hair in a classic chignon, sipping an espresso. She watched my husband move in his long red kimono as if he was the center of a Noh drama. Yes, she hummed, and now she was looking at me, saying, Such a cute girl. I smiled, she smiled back. I winked, she looked startled. I told her the story of the baby fawn that appeared in the cottage the night I was born.

Speckled? she asked. Freckled! I said, no need to point out the constellation that covered my nose and cheeks. She's perfect, said Dewi to my husband. I'll put on some clothes, he said.

But neither Betsy nor Dewi showed up at my surprise nineteenth birthday party at the Jakarta Hilton. Dewi obviously I didn't know well, but Betsy would have been the best surprise of all. In the center salon of the penthouse, which occupied the entire top of the main building, an orchestra, with both Western and gamelan playlists, blasted tunes from a raised marble plinth. There was plenty of room but the music was mildly deafening so the party assembled on the covered wraparound terraces as wide as freeways. And also in the head-of-state dining room. Some sat for earnest conversation in deep leather bucket chairs in the long library, which had not a single book on the elaborately carved shelves. It's worth saying that everything in Jakarta is elaborately carved. My husband explained the economics of woodwork. The cocktail bar of the Jakarta Hilton, for instance, had required more artisan laborers than St. Peter's Basilica in Rome. But they finished the whole thing in three weeks, not three centuries!

In the penthouse there was a back bedroom draped in various silks, large swooping swaths of fabric, held back, just barely, by silver dragon curlicues. There were actually four of these bedrooms, color coded. I chose red for the power of my birthday, and sat on the bed to make a phone call to Betsy back in good old Tokyo. No one would miss me at the party. No one actually knew me. Except Mustache who'd been hired to sit in a small chair by the front door doing nothing. The hotel operator was very polite, and when I told him my name, said, Happy Birthday, Fawn! Still, he regretted he could not connect my call. Party rules.

It was dull at my party. Loud and dull. And once the cake was served and I'd posed for the photographs and I'd obligingly tongued some red strawberry icing along my husband's new dental work, I was free to wander. I wandered to the front door and tried to leave. Mustache sprung to his feet. No, Mrs. Fawn, more surprise coming soon.

Yes, Mustache, I know that. I'd adopted a tone of absolute dominance, which is the basic how-to of talking to a servant in Jakarta. Betsy would faint, laugh maybe, then faint. But it was the protocol. Mustache and I were friends. In a mystical no-communication kind of way, I think now, looking back.

Mrs. Fawn, he said, bowing, but I could see his machete tucked into the block-print vest he wore—textiles, another burgeoning economy here—and something else bulged under his armpit. I smiled, I couldn't help it. He whispered, really to himself, because addressing me directly was out of the question. Poor Mrs. Fawn, he whispered, and then began to shout at a passing waiter in a language I would never learn. I knew all about diversion, as a fashion model it was my profession. So I slipped out of the party to see if I could call Betsy on a pay phone in the coffee shop. She would definitely remember my birthday, hers was only two days later. We'd done sixteen and seventeen together, eighteen we missed because of my honeymoon on Khashoggi's yacht—so crowded, no phones. But at nineteen we could wish each other well, we were grown-ups. The world was changing at our feet. By now she might have an old American of her own; if not, well, there are worse things than trading complaints with Hec!

Just for fun, I took the emergency staircase. My legs, even with the twins poking their way out of my belly, were still as okay as ever. Get the Fawn! For almost a whole year I was in every single beverage ad in all of Japan that involved a leg shot. Not just Tokyo, I mean everywhere! I froze my fanny off posing in hot pants and skis on Mount Fuji, but it was all necessary. Contrast, everyone understood, contrast is what sold. The biggest contrast in Jakarta is between the rich, who hang out at the Hilton, and the poor, who live in cardboard lean-tos stacked against the chain-link construction fence, because every day the Hilton gets bigger.

The coffee shop on the lobby level had recently become pink, which is why normally my instinct would have been to avoid it. Although pink is believed to be almost universally flattering, Betsy and I discovered one late night, with some hilarious experimental pubic hair dying, that pink didn't work with my skin. Too much, she paused, too much, and decided on a nice silvery blue instead. Just the thing for your geriatric. Fortunately that stuff washes right out, so he never saw it. I didn't want to make him feel I was mocking him. Talk about a thin skin!

Up until my birthday at the Hilton I never really took guns seriously, they were just an ornament to set the tone the way a good pair of false eyelashes could rearrange an expression straight from tired to joy. Tokyo wasn't exactly dangerous in the Roppongi district but sometimes at parties, and in the suites afterward, there'd be some blue hardware lying around creating a mood. A mood, let me say, I liked! And so did Betsy, it sort of pushed us out of ourselves in a way that redesigning our pubic hair couldn't. And as professionals we limited our drugs. Quaaludes, Valium, okay. Heroin, any variation on cocaine—and there was a lot around—bad for business. I like to think that's what attracted my old American, my professional discipline—Betsy's, too—and then to single me out, my legs.

In the coffee shop I was scouting around for the pay phone that just last week I could swear was right beside the candy counter when I noticed the four identical guys in textile vests blocking all the elevators. I'd been right to take the stairs! I inserted myself between some free-floating banquettes before anyone else could get picky about the birthday rules.

Although the Hilton was usually the hot spot for foreign investors and expats, the place had been cleared for my party. No one spun through the cathedral-height doors complaining about their luggage still stuck in Kuala Lumpur. This Hilton had a direct line to the baggage carousel in the Malaysian airport I would come to know so well. But today, no lost anything, no outraged arrivals. The great glass doors were sealed and the men by the elevators were gluing their eyes to the twelve guys by the entrance in demimilitary gear, scarcely the thing for a summer party—hot!—and their guns were mood killers. Nothing sexy about those black toaster ovens hanging down from shoulder straps. Not even a festive bullet belt. Somehow that was more of a downer, the idea that all the bullets they would ever need were already loaded.

I had to go to the bathroom in the sudden emergency style that comes over pregnant people. I shimmied toward the ladies room and managed, for the first time in my life, to capture no one's attention. Betsy was completely right about pink! Like you're not even there! she said, and usually that was a big liability.

It was old-fashioned in the bathroom, and as I sat and pondered the surprising security detail of my birthday party I thought about my husband with such nostalgia, as if I already sensed the future. He meant well. The whole subservience thing just a personality glitch. My own mother was a problem for me in that way. Either devote your life to me and my wishes, or die. Those were my Denmark options. So Betsy sold her family's only car (they were surprised!) and we lit out for Tokyo where Western-style models are popular, especially blondes. My god, I sent my mother so many presents, but she never responded. Betsy had some ideas about this, and when I first met my old American, she said, Just call him Mommy! Maybe she repeated this at the party. Maybe that's why she got the boot. I do miss Betsy. She always said what was on her mind. What would she say to see me loitering in a bathroom that looked like an overstocked showroom. White marble pedestal sinks and satin-wrapped chaises by the dozen.

But the one thing the Indonesian laborers got all wrong, as hard and fast as they worked—and so cheap!—was the idea of privacy. Apparently it was untranslatable, no word in the language, that's what my husband said. And it pissed him off to no end. They liked sleeping stacked together like lumber. They liked doors that never closed. They liked more doors not closing per room than people to pass through them. And so, as with every room here at the sprawling Hilton, this one had several exits. At least two of them led to the outdoor pavilion surrounding the wishing fountain and the pool.

Probably my biggest professional problem is the tendency of my skin to burn like toast. Really quick. But the pavilion was shady, so that was good. And quiet, as if the deafening happiness of my party flew up into the sky and took all the noise of the world with it. Here in the swimming arena only the gurgle of the wishing fountain and the buzz of the automatic insect remover made a sound. No birds, no workmen keeping world-record schedules; everyone and everything off duty for my birthday.

The pool was a suspicious shade of lavender, something to do with salt and alkaline something or other, but it looked so cool, so inviting. And the twins were heavy in the heat. I shimmied out of my birthday dress and under things and made a giant splash entry into the deep end. My husband wouldn't mind if the party leaned over the edge of the wraparound terrace and saw me. It was just part of my general charm: free-spirited, pregnant with sons, very blonde. But no one looked, and the terrace thirty stories up was as remote and quiet as a fortress in a movie when everyone inside knows the enemy is hiding in the shrubbery.

Sometimes swimming makes me feel like a baby myself, less at the compound because everything was familiar, but here at the Hilton in a pool meant to exercise an Olympic team someday, I floated around and felt my baby self, cuddled down in a sleep hammock, ignored by my mother who was smoking a cigarette and thinking dark thoughts. This is a story I tell Betsy all the time. Oh, no, she says, here it comes, the maternal dodge.

Not so! No, I just understood early that I wasn't exactly the pip of her universe. I mean, I'm a realist! I was a realist baby!

Yeah, yeah, said Betsy, hold still. And she applied a hot but pleasantly scented wax to my inner thighs. Jasmine? I asked.

Yuck, she said.

Sometimes I think it's that realist bent that made things go the way they did later on. When Mustache kept telling me that any moment the phone service would return to the compound and I might even get a passport, well, I knew a fib when I heard one. But that's all later, and the part I'm talking about—the part Betsy would call the shriveled nut—happens in the pool. I like to think I made a choice that day, and maybe even a good one.

I was bobbing around in the shady water where the pergola imitates the Parthenon, only in wood. The twins settled into their natural element and stopped pressing into my kidneys. This floating strategy would come in handy as time went on. At the compound whenever they played the recording of my old American saying that dumb stuff about the photo albums, the twins would get all aggressive, so I'd flop into the pool and float until they calmed down. And Mustache just had to wait. Had to cultivate a little patience if he thought I was going to sit there and look at my husband's first, second, and third wives, again, for the eightieth time. And all their expensive daughters. I got so tired of the albums. And Betsy predicted it. You may be the Big Now, for now, she said, but just wait.

Wait for what?

The marriage merge: he won't know who's who. He'll be calling you Helga, and the bad part? You'll be answering. So sad.

How did she even know there was a Helga? Betsy is uncanny that way. If only she'd been there. She'd have known what Mustache needed to find in the albums in a snap.

But on my birthday I was twirling around in the Hilton pool, eyes closed, feeling just like I was back in Denmark, in the creek in our yard, doing a dead-body-style swim to scare my mother. Easy to do, very slow breaths, no bubbles allowed, limbs loose and wavy in the water. I'd squint open a half lid to check, but my mother would be smoking and staring at her hand, not a bit concerned. I'd climb out onto the bank where she sat. So you can float, she said, a turd can float.

Not really, I said, and she slapped me. But why think of this at my party. Except that in a flash in the shady end of the Hilton pool I knew I could float or sink, pretend to be alive or dead, and no one could make the comment to grab and squash the pip of my heart ever again. I'd grown up for good. And I opened my eyes, thinking I should find my old American and tell him my insight. But instead, lounging in a disrespectful way by the pool side, was Mustache. And he'd borrowed one of the toaster-oven guns from the guys in the military costumes. He still wore his party vest, which I preferred.

I don't need guarding, I growled. Go away, Mustache. I'm happy on my own.

Happy birthday, Mrs. Fawn! Please choose to dress now. Surprise finished. He made what might be an Indonesian hand gesture of celebration. I really don't know. But what was most obvious was that he was wearing my husband's watch. A ridiculous gold Bulgari that always embarrassed me. But it was a gift and that's all that mattered to my old American. He was all about gifts. Dewi Sukarno went home that long-ago Tokyo morning with his red silk kimono in a shopping bag. There was some mysterious language at work here. Me? He gave me the gift of himself, which after a while became more and more perplexing. I like diamonds, but I didn't get any. It was strange. Don't spoil her! said Dewi Sukarno, lifting her large pocketbook, waving a diminutive farewell. She's perfect just as she is. Well, what would she think if she saw me with the twin belly, and the sunburn that's become permanent? The whole time we were stuck in the compound, Mustache refused to refill my prescription sunblock. It was not essential. Not what Betsy would say! But Mustache, from the start, was a very different kind of roommate.

Is it worth saying my mother was unconcerned with my fair skin, too? She was quite dark herself, my father must have been albino to make up the difference, and the question only got me a dislocated arm. So temperamental. Betsy said there were other words for it, but I refused to listen. My husband was right, Betsy could be fanciful about people's ordinary habits. For instance, on our first date, Betsy came along, and he got

spectacularly high, stole a car—from a friend so it wasn't actually stealing—and drove it all the way to the Ginza section,
pie-eyed, before hitting a news- stand. Demolishing the intricate fan pattern of the international glossies. Death wish, she
called it. And maybe he heard her and took it the wrong way.
But she was actually talking to me. I realize that now. She hadn't
really liked my old American. Morose, she called him, in fact,
psychotic.

He's reflective, I said, you just don't recognize a thinker when
you see one.

Mustache was a thinker. After all the birthday security moved
into our compound, whenever I woke up in the middle of the
night—guaranteed with the twins—in the master suite Mustache was always awake. Even curled on the mat at the foot of
the vast carved bed, his eyes were wide open as if I might dream
myself up the twenty-foot wall and free.

Mustache, I'd say, stepping over him, feeling my way to the
loo, I don't like you that way. And by then I was only lying
slightly. That mat used to be mine. My husband thought it
incredibly sexy if I slept there. Up and going to the bathroom
for old-guy reasons, he would trip over me and then wow! he'd
have fun!

Why subject yourself to that shit, Betsy asked on the phone,
back when I could call her.

It's nothing, I said.

I'll say.

Every day Mustache made a big promise to turn the electricity back on, and with it, the central AC, like he was the boss. Which, it turns out, he was! But I'd stopped believing him, even if he did make a mean rice and mango on the propane burner in the servant hut. I wasn't allowed in there because his wife, mother, sisters, and daughters would all be tainted by me. But every once in a while they'd peek out the slits between the boards to get a look-see.

Won't they be tainted by all those guys with the toaster ovens stomping around here day and night? I asked.

Oh, Mrs. Fawn, sighed Mustache.

Did I say you could sigh?

He bowed his head, but we were just goofing around. And it was about a thousand degrees and the marble floors felt like one big hot plate. Who had the energy for dominance talk to put people back in their rightful place?

It's all about energy. This is what my old American used to say, though he was thinking globally, and it's what Stefan said in the letter he wrote to me in Tokyo.

What a putz, said Betsy, and I would have laughed at the word, so odd from her, but I was crying and just wanted the letter back. My mother didn't have the energy to fight, that's what Stefan wrote. Some kid broke into our cottage on the creek, thinking it was abandoned. She never did like to mow the lawn, or fix a single thing. I guess the kid screamed when he saw her and my mother lay down on the floor, just like that. The next minute she was dead. Heart, Stefan said, exploded like a grenade. She didn't really care for life that much, didn't have the energy for it. On any level. If you know what I mean.

Fucking Stefan, said Betsy, but it didn't help.

In some ways Mustache really reminds me of Stefan, skinny and bent over and worried all the time. It's more than just the tainted daughters. He sounded pretty pro forma on that: Your whorish filth, Mrs. Fawn, that's all it is. Like saying your freckles might be contagious. He smiles, I smile, we know it's all nonsense, and if the guys in every room and lounging like idiots on the wall tops and by every single door had cracked a smile now and then, too, it would have been a lot more pleasant. I'm not the problem, I'd say to Mustache, and nod, subtly, toward one of the minigoons. Not a single one as tall as I am. Betsy could break them in two with a look.

Sometimes when I tripped over him in the night, I could tell he'd been crying, or at least sweating very hard. What is it, Mustache? I'd ask, but he never answered me. Go to sleep, Mrs. Fawn. Sleep now.

But one night, after about a month of this, much too long for anything by Indonesian standards—and when, I wanted to know, would I see the American ob-gyn who lived at the Hilton?— there was a big crash from the salon, followed by louder crashes and howls, as if tiny ones were tossing around all the carved furniture. Mustache was already at the doors, sliding in various bolts, so that now we were locked in and the air was thick with our sleep breath and sweat. Oh, Mustache, I said, and felt a jerk of the babies under my heart. Bile rippled in my throat and I thought I might pee in my nightie. Please, Mustache, unbolt the loo, now, please.

One minute, Mrs. Fawn, and he listened closely through one thick embellished door, and even in the half-light of a new moon I could see he was trembling and most certainly crying.

I think the news for your husband not positive.

I shook my head, almost not understanding. Mustache and I never talked about my husband anymore, except to listen to that old recording and plod through the photo albums, but we hadn't even done that in forever.

Oh, they're just goofing around.

No, said Mustache. Not goofing, Mrs. Fawn. Where would we like to hide you now.

I need a toilet, Mustache.

And that seemed to give him an idea, but one that caused him some distress.

When we first moved to Jakarta, my old American used to say he didn't like the design of this compound. He thought, he insisted, and not in a happy, life-is-wild-and-unpredictable way, that the servants watched us in the night. Well, he was absolutely right! And that's something that people would say about him later on at the strange memorial service in baggage claim at Kuala Lumpur. That he was always one step ahead of the game. In fact, he was ahead of his time. He was history in the making. He was a national treasure. Obviously a national tragedy. He was the lesson that could never be learned well enough. But he was also a state secret. He would be missed more than anyone would ever be free to say.

He also had another wife, and only one, who, though devastated, couldn't make it to Kuala Lumpur. There were documents to prove we were never actually married. And if I ever intended to leave the sour smelling, ill-lit annex to the baggage Quonset hut, only my own country could help me now. The Americans were finished with me. But this was far down the road, and in the moment I like to remember as tender in its way, Mustache was struggling to release the heavy center panel of the twenty-foot-long carved wooden screen depicting the many-headed goddesses of desire. The spectacular backdrop for my husband's king-sized marital fib and my rustic floor mat.

It turned out I wasn't the only one my old American hadn't been strictly truthful with. Poor Mustache had received many promises: about his daughters being educated at Harvard, and the strong likelihood of ponies for everyone on a farm in Connecticut. For such a smart man, I'm surprised Mustache believed him, but look at me. And Mustache did look at me, and what he saw, apparently, was some merger of all those women who would naturally be corroded to the very pip of their beings by the sight of me. They see you all the time, he admitted. His wife knew some good herbs to keep the twins from punching my lungs.

The floors in the compound always seemed to have more gravity than other floors I'd encountered and in my idle hours I had time to consider why. It was the weight of the marble slabs. It was the heavy burdens of the day laborers that had seeped into the porous layers. It was my imagination, maybe. But I don't think so. Betsy always said I had a fatality imagination. Not that I foresaw the worst, the opposite: I saw love and opportunity in every future, and that was fatal. So Mustache's daughters—huddled that final night around the Bunsen burner in the servant hut—struck me as graceful and potential model material wherever mottle-skinned emaciated models were in demand. And his wife, though her face was stricken on one side, had delighted eyes, even cast down, even shooing me into a corner to wait for the gunfire to die down so we could all crawl out a dirt tunnel to the relative safety of the airport.

I was accustomed to downcast eyes, they followed me everywhere in Indonesia. When my husband's assistant, Kartini, arrived one day out of the blue—this was the day before my birthday party—she gave Mustache, who was seated by the front door, guarding me, which had always been his main job, some elaborate instructions.

What is it, Kartini? I called out. But she smiled and bowed and continued to speak very quickly before handing a thick envelope to Mustache. She bowed again, eyes sideways and staring as usual. What time is my husband coming home? I asked.

So busy, Mrs. Fawn. Terrible busy. Very sorry. Have a nice day! And my husband's work chauffeur drove her back to the office.

It turned out I was going to Borobudur in Yogyakarta that very afternoon as a special prebirthday treat. Good sights! said Mustache with averted eyes. We would leave for the airport as soon as I could pack my bag.

The biggest shock, when I first arrived in Jakarta from Tokyo, was the contrasting airports. In Tokyo, no matter who drives you to the airport, you are guaranteed a new lace doily for your headrest. And probably some artfully packaged snacks and beverages, and the airport was equally tidy and efficient. In Jakarta, arriving and departing passengers mill through chain fences and pens with padlocks and razor wire. Anyone can carry a machine gun if they feel like it. So if someone motions you over with a gun snout it could be customs, it could be a holdup. They are very disorganized. And even though the airport in Tokyo is a million miles from the city, the highways, like everything else, are immaculate and gorgeously lit. In Jakarta, the airport is practically next door, and you have to be inside it to see it's not another shack selling scary fruit water off a pitted dirt road. Only in the end, with Mustache, did I understand how good a system that was.

But the day we traveled to Borobudur I was still appalled by the disorganization. Some thug in a luggage-handling basement patted my belly and said something foul—I could tell from his eyes, and the screwy shape of his mouth, and the aroma of sour melon. What did he say? I asked Mustache.

He says we pay extra for the little passengers. No mind, Mrs. Fawn. And Mustache withdrew a document from the thick envelope, which quickly had this baggage handler looking anxious. Right away we were led out a side door, past the overflowing trash bins, old oil barrels filled with fish heads and sewage. I thought I might be very sick, and the twins were outraged, but Mustache fanned my face with the envelope then raced ahead. Please, Mrs. Fawn. We hurry now.

Soon we were standing on the tarmac before a small plane decorated with palm-tree camouflage. Mustache called up to the pilot, who was leaning out the window of the cockpit smoking a clove cigarette. He looked at me, swerved away his eyes, then a steward lowered a snaky looking gangplank. First class, please, he announced in English. We were the only passengers. I sat in a padded bucket behind the pilot, and Mustache sat on the floor at the rear of the plane next to several metal trunks and my Burberry overnight tote.

It was a very short trip, which was fortunate. The pilot smoked the entire way, and told jokes that made him hee-haw and cough to whoever sat on the other end of his radio. The plane bobbed and dipped and finally made an abrupt landing in the middle of a rice terrace. There were no handlers or even a hut to receive us, but Mustache barked out something to the pilot, and the steward appeared again—where had he ridden?—to lower the gangplank. Once outside the plane, I could clear my eyes of smoke and look around me. So beautiful, greens that were almost turquoise. Water falling through wooden trellises more lavender than the Hilton swimming pool, and a smell beyond the cloud of clove cigarettes as soft and kind as a mother's love. That gentle, that embracing. What mother are you referring to, that's what Betsy would horn in with, if she'd been there. But this is how I'll be to the twins, like this air, I remember thinking. Blue and beautiful and puffy with love.

Mustache said we would come back for my tote, first we must see Borobudur. He apologized for leading the way then bid me follow him down the path. We stopped by a small carved altar in the rock; three stone women looked into our faces. Mustache scrambled off the path and returned with a white flower. Ask for guidance, Mrs. Fawn, all will come. He gave me something sweeter smelling than the wax Betsy used on my inner thighs. There now, I said, and placed the white flower near their splayed stone toes and waited for thoughts I might recognize as more interesting than my own. I closed my eyes and stood still.

Maybe later, Mrs. Fawn, said Mustache. Please, Mrs. Fawn.

I didn't realize we were in a rush, but now Mustache moved faster. At the end of the path, at the bottom of the lowest rice terrace, a group of men stood waiting. The same group, by the way, that would completely spoil my party. They seemed to know Mustache, in fact seemed a tiny bit intimidated, which was very strange. Mustache spoke in the fast loud style he never used with me, and showed them some papers from the fat envelope. Most of the men scurried up the path we'd just left, but two followed us, now at a respectful distance, to the car waiting in the dirt track. It was a taxi. Or had once been a taxi. Private car now, explained Mustache. And opened the back door on a loose hinge. Please use seat belt for safety, Mrs. Fawn. Mustache rode beside the driver. And the two men who'd joined us stood on the back fender and held onto the roof. Their brown wire fingers wrapped around the tops of the open back windows. We were going to Borobudur.

I don't like the word hostage, it sounds very passive, like nothing is going on inside to the person involved. Although the Americans in Kuala Lumpur use that word a lot. They insist this prebirthday sightseeing was an essential link to what occurred later at my party, that in effect I was prekidnapped. But I feel certain that's not what happened to me. I was always alive to my surroundings. Awake! Aware! Alive! That's what my old American used to say, something to do with good posture. It's almost impossible to believe he is none of those things anymore.

Borobudur was in terrible disrepair, and the snack bar had been set on fire not so long ago. The charred-wood smell still wafted from black sooty puddles. Snipped coils of razor wire blew around in the hot wind like tumbleweed. Nothing was left to protect. Vandals, said Mustache, shaking his head. Disrespect, Mrs. Fawn. He bowed his head. Then he said the most important thing to do immediately was to climb the temple walk, counterclockwise, until I reached the top, then go inside a big Buddha head and look around. I'll wait here, said Mustache.

I frowned.

Thank you, Mrs. Fawn, he said.

I sighed. All right. But I was beginning to be hungry. After this, lunch, Mustache, and right away, I said in my harshest tone. He handed me a leaf-wrapped ball from a hidden vest pocket. This was the first time I tasted the mango rice that was to become my steady diet.

Someday they would clean all this up. Money was pouring into Indonesia and there was lots of talk about the ancient culture and the importance of art and respect for religion, but for the moment sludge and weeds choked the counterclockwise walkway, bits and pieces of the temple lay shattered everywhere. I stepped over shards in my inappropriate platform sandals, determined to show Mustache that my legs were more than just decoration. Did he ever think about my legs? Apparently he did. But not the way Betsy would have suspected. He wanted his daughters to live and grow to have long strong legs like mine, that's what he said in the end. Maybe still, Mrs. Fawn, you can help us.

And I keep telling the Americans that the only reason I'm able to help *them* at all is because Mustache and his family saved me. They're deaf to this idea; they've never heard of Mustache, they say. And besides, how exactly do I think I've been helpful? I want to see an ob-gyn? Maybe I'll give birth to the information they're looking for, hmm? Maybe a little unassisted labor will shake my memory loose.

But what I'm really trying to remember, what I want to get right, is the moment I finally reached the top of Borobudur. It was early afternoon but already the sun had dipped behind a nearby mountain so the light on the littered flattop was filtered green through the swaying trees. A mist in the air landed on my skin like a cool astringent, something Betsy might pull out of our picnic-basket-sized refrigerator to put on our cheeks on August nights on our tatami mat. This air and the sad shape of the vast Buddha heads with their beaded hairdos made me long to go home, just that. But not to Denmark; I'd already told Stefan he could have the cottage by the creek. He'd probably trimmed the wild overgrown hedges into topiary by now waiting for me to return and take my rightful place. No, I wanted to be with Betsy in Tokyo, and inside the only Buddha head that hadn't been toppled or riddled with gunshot, I looked out through the slit of the eyes and imagined our future. I would call her on my birthday. I would come home, with the twins of course, and together we would rethink our whole plan, start over. I knew what she'd say, Your geezer will never let you escape! And

I'd say, He has no hold on me. And she would be impressed by my new maturity. And chances are we'd be very conservative with our appearance for a while, just while the glue dried on our new life. That's what I saw, and then I looked down and spotted Mustache by the burned-out snackbar waving madly, his new friends slipping in and out beneath the palm trees. They had all seen me and soon they would reunite at my birthday party. Now they could drift out into the forests if they felt like it. That fluid, unpredictable style of friendship really irked my old American. No word for loyalty, he said, on more than one occasion. But later I found out he was wrong about that, something my new Americans refuse to understand. Hey, hey! I could see the shape of Mustache's mouth calling, and it looked sweet with affection for me. But at the top of Borobudur the only sound I could hear inside the Buddha head and inside my very pip was the tiny, swirling, shifting breeze of certainty and peace.

Double Happiness

THE OUTER OFFICE WAS MUCH THE SAME AS SHE REMEM-
bered it. Mrs. Guski's thick, neat oak desk, a manageable stack
of buff folders in the far right corner. A small red-haired boy
in a blazer knocked unhappy heels against the chair leg. He'd
been waiting for a while, a path of tears nearly dry on his freckled cheek.

Ann McCleary had boys of her own, long grown; boys she'd
left to stew in that very chair. Her line: If you got yourself there,
you'd done something to deserve it. She'd made a single ex-
ception with Terry, age seven, when a polished oxford lace-up
went skidding under the desks to catch the attention of a girl
he favored. Even younger, even in nursery school, Terry had
some tiny sweetheart stilled to contemplation, to watching
him. She smiled to think of him, not the handsomest of her
boys, but the one, the one who lit up the room.

Terry and his flying shoe; his father just in the grave a month,
and he was making trouble. She'd come down to this very office,

to Sister Mary Arthur who was nearly a girl then herself, a young woman with large responsibilities. Ann McCleary had appreciated her qualities from the start, the kindness, the steely discipline that made her a deft judge of the foibles of others. Terry still as a stone, not kicking the edges of the chair leg, face turned down, the brown eye that wandered inward when he was upset wandered now, and Ann gave him the look, then retracted it. She remembered that like something physical, pulling back and seeing the situation for what it was. Dear heart, she'd said, just out of Mrs. Guski's hearing, let me speak to Sister.

And Mary Arthur needed little enlightenment, they understood each other without much conversation. Just this once, Ann McCleary took one of her children—there were five in all, the last born only months before she lost her beloved Dan—just this once she'd intervened between cause and effect. Off to the Dairy Queen, then home where he watched *One Life to Live* while she ironed, and then *Dark Shadows* with his brothers when they came home from school. His sister, Kathleen, demanded an explanation. Hands on her hips, already the litigator, always fierce for justice. He's sad, explained Ann to her only daughter.

We're all sad, said Kathleen.

Give me a kiss. Ann set the iron on its trivet, reached both hands to smooth back the bangs, grown in too long, that blocked her daughter's blue eyes. What did you hear about your grand project, is it to be Argentina or Brazil?

* * *

Mrs. Guski never fooled with color in her hair, unlike so many in Holy Cross parish with frosted bobs. We're all becoming beach-blanket blondes, said Ann McCleary on more than one occasion, but Mrs. Guski had given up. Even the nuns, the young ones especially, did better. And Mary Arthur had always been elegant, her shining hair cut by an expensive hand. She was the public face of Holy Cross and no one begrudged her the care, the handsome suits or the good shoes, not the way they did Father's vintage Karmann Ghia, a disgrace and an embarrassment.

But not an indecent man, really, and a fancy car was a small thing after all; he knew when to hide it away. And he'd backed her up when she'd said she wanted a funeral, no more waiting. I can't wait anymore, she'd said. And Father Jim Rielly understood, and two Saturdays later pulled down the garage door in the early morning and went in the side porch to the sacristy to make sure his best purple vestments were ready, and of course they were. Monmouth County was especially hard hit, New Jersey struck almost as if the towers had stood on its side of the river. But only two from Rumson, it turned out, and this was about affluence and influence some said. Who with any pull would take an office there? But Terry hadn't felt that way at all. So Ann McCleary knew influence and affluence were just part of the endless chatter. He'd come down for Sunday supper, a rare appearance, not like her other boys with tow-heads and pregnant wives. Girls who'd been so ambitious now trailed toddlers through her beds and borders, breast-fed on the screened-in porch as if the neighbors were blind, and dumb. Terry, busy with business and still unsure about settling down, a favorite with his nieces and nephews, gave each a card with his new office address, just moved in. Views to Kansas, he said, to California, even, astonishing. They would all go visit, he said they must, and from his desk survey the world.

The Rumson police, the Little Silver police, the Middletown police especially insisted; they'd already had funerals of their own and knew what to expect. The roads were cordoned off from the Sea Bright Bridge to the Avenue of Two Rivers and cars parked for a mile all the way down Rumson Road. Women in black sling-backs climbing the rutted grass along the road made the shortcut through the tennis club across the school yard to the gray shingle church, capacity four hundred; someone said a thousand stood inside and out to hear Father Jim say no words could gather the force he needed to say his prayer, they would all join him in silence. Kathleen in the choir loft, alone, sang "Danny Boy" for her brother, for her father, and the thousand beyond prayer, beyond tears, shook and trembled now.

Her mother had said, No, not that, meaning the dress of black chiffon. It's not a cocktail party. At the house, just before, they all snapped at one another. The toddlers wept and no one could decide who would be the one to drive their mother.

In the end she'd ridden with Kathleen who knew when to be still, unlike the boys, hugging her too hard, clutching at her hand. Boys were the bigger saps, she'd always known. Kathleen could drive without talking and she knew how to get through a police barrier without making the well-intentioned feel like fools.

Sister Mary Arthur must have been there, must have been crucial and efficient, and would have come to the club later, all were invited, encouraged to gather by the water where the boats rocked in the small cove and cleats on sails knocked a beautiful music across the treetops, last of their dusty green. Early October, soon the leaves would be down and the boats in dry dock, she couldn't have waited another moment. She wore black, none of this nonsense of color for her. Though many in yellows even, and blues. Sister Mary Arthur would know to wear mourning, but Ann McCleary had no memory of her at all that day. She saw Kathleen in her cocktail dress, which suited her, truth be told, bare-legged and barefoot in a dinghy with one of the Henderson boys, the one who saw it all, he claimed, from the Staten Island ferry. Long ride, said Ann. Excuse me, Mrs. McCleary? You saw it all, it must have been a very long ride. She was a stickler for exact speech. She was toggled far from sense with grief. Both versions arrived on dinner tables sooner or later. All admired her for going ahead, for deciding to acknowledge the loss when so many were waiting, and for what?

Her daughter Kathleen was thirty-five years old the day her brother likely died. At first they thought if anyone could survive, it would be Terry. They pictured him and the several others he'd no doubt been able to rally, rushing out of the falling ash, rowing to safety. They said it out loud, lifted up with the knowledge of his character, what would surely keep him, and anyone fortunate enough to be in his vicinity, safe. Kathleen had combed the city for the first sign. Not giving up. Even when her mother said, Come home, dear heart. Please. A little girl when she lost her father, Terry nearly seven and never to be a father himself, or a husband. Never had the chance, she'd overheard near the water, over the clang of the boats, the same wineglass still in her hand—Eat something, Mom—she caught the sob. Never wanted to be either, said Ann, he had no example to follow. And who's fault was that. Only her own. Only mine, she said, when asked.

Ann McCleary, said Sister Mary Arthur, smiling, stepping out of her sunny office, arms open by the hips, chest lifted, an unconscious mimicry of the gentle open arms of the Virgin. Come in. She gave an even glance to the miscreant in the chair, sighed. Come in, Mrs. McCleary; Ann, please.

Ann had a job in mind, and Sister heard her out. She listened and nodded and said, Let me think about this a bit?

Of course, yes, said Ann McCleary, standing. This was quick, and now in her mortification, it wasn't what she was expecting. She'd grown used to a certain deference, people let her ahead of them in any line. And all the rest she didn't like to believe she noticed, because for so long she hadn't. Now to perceive her privilege was to have survived, and that was unthinkable.

You were good to take the time, she said.

Please, said Sister Mary Arthur, with the composure to stand quite still, to not glance at her desk or lean toward the side door, toward her next task. Please, she said, let's speak soon.

What did that mean? Ann McCleary who understood everything, who never needed any human utterance interpreted or explained. On her way out, she looked down at the little redhead knocking his heels and thought, at least he knows what he's doing here.

So she wasn't waiting for the call that evening. Not a bit. She was nursing a glass of red wine for her heart, though wine hadn't saved her husband's young heart from failing. She was nibbling a scrap of cheese on a Triscuit when the phone rang and it was Sister Mary Arthur explaining her need for a lower-school library. A vision, she said. One I've harbored for years.

A terrible thought went through Ann McCleary's mind, even Sister Mary Arthur was after her imagined millions. And they were imaginary, though the papers went on about them. That, and everything else, the construction nonsense, the bullhorn the president picked up and to her mind never put down, and for what. She went with Kathleen and the boys, but not their wives or their children, to stand in the frightening pit, to walk through cordons of police and to look up into the empty sky, and she waited. Waited for someone to say something she could listen to. Someone had mentioned the smell. Was it one of her boys? But she couldn't sense a thing. She was waiting to hear someone who wouldn't lie to her. But she knew the cost of that kind of speech because she'd seen it happen, once. But first, they'd stood in line at the Armory on Lexington to give up his hairbrush and the business card Terry had been so proud to hand to the babies, who chewed on them. Don't worry, Mom, they're engraved! Feel.

They'd gone down into the dark stone underground and waited as the lists were turned again and again, empty pages from the city examiner, from the morgue. Who thought to place them here in the cold stone room, airless. Kathleen unwrapped a protein bar from the checkered basket of a volunteer. Eat, Mom, please.

On the third day, Terry's company set up a center for the families at a midtown hotel. Black slick elevators coursed up the high tower to the rooms dimly lit, a false lemon fragrance in the air. The Internet. The phone banks. The food, constantly refreshed: pancakes, steaks, any kind of eggs. Like Easter, said Ann. And Kathleen said, Maybe we should go home. But she wanted to hear what the CEO had to say. So they went with the others, over a hundred, maybe two hundred. Who could count. And they sat in a tiered room, round tables with blue tablecloths, pads and pens. The microphones were difficult to adjust. Men in suits skipped up the sidelines and back and whispered to clumps of other suited men with heads down, hands in pockets.

They'd heard bits and pieces. They all knew about the stairwells now. They all had maps of the area, and diagrams of the buildings, they knew which elevators stopped on which segment and which went to the top. They had a sense of timing and possibility. They'd been tracking these things for days. Two days now. And on the third, the microphone settled finally into a stand, a man grayer than the rest broke free and said, after running a thumb across the mesh and hearing the purr, the crackle: I'm the chief executive officer and I'd like to tell you what I know. He said, Anyone who arrived at work on Monday—

Already the hands were in the air. How could they know? How could they know, was there a list somewhere, an attendance list perhaps? Something that could be distributed?

He said, and first he coughed, he said that he would try to find something like that but this is what they knew so far, that no one, not a single person who arrived at work, who made it above the seventy-second floor, who made the change and climbed into the second elevator, not a single person who arrived at work that day had survived. Not one. If they came to work, if they arrived. No one. Not a single one. Not anyone.

All around the ballroom hands shot up. What about staircase A? And what about the walls that were only Sheetrock, easily penetrated, easily torn through. The man at the microphone pushed down the large black bulb near his mouth and sobbed. And the hands stayed in the air, some polite, all waiting for his composure to reassert itself. She was the only person in the room that believed him. She watched him for another minute. Let's go, she said to Kathleen. Outside the ballroom she waited, opening her purse to see that she still had her wallet, she'd been so forgetful lately. She waited while Kathleen called the boys, who would be in Rumson already, looking for pots and pans. She waited another week, then called Father Rielly, and he said, Of course, Ann, of course. She was grateful that he hadn't felt the least impulse to offer his counsel.

It was a miracle Sister Mary Arthur got through at all, the way Kathleen monopolized the phone. Set up in her old bedroom, taking her time to sort out her next move. She'd left the perfectly good law firm behind to think about NGOs. She told her mother, There's so much I could be doing! So far, the doing involved tying up her mother's telephone lines and flirting with the Henderson boy. Whose wife everyone knew was a grave disappointment, according to Kathleen. Who says, Ann McCleary asked, what's to be disappointed about these days? Everything preset, preknown. No surprises. And her daughter gave her the look she'd grown weary of in herself, the no-point-explaining look. There it is, the family crest, said Ann. She put a hand to her daughter's cheek. We must learn some new tricks, you and I. And that's why she'd gone to see Sister Mary Arthur. She needed to expand, she needed new experience or she'd die. Not that dying had been out of the question. She'd realized, after a long while, her own proclivity to slip away. And that understanding might have had something to do with Kathleen and the lovely suits piled up on the twin bed, and the job search that went nowhere.

First the fall, the kind of slip anyone might take, a spill off a high wet slate step. But she'd hit her head and her chest, a bruise spreading over her left side, blue as a sign from God. Something holy. Advil helped and was all she agreed to take, along with a bit of wine past five. That was the first winter. In spring she walked out to pick a flower, a daffodil, and was bit by something nearly malarial. High fevers and her gait grew rigid from the inflammation. But she didn't understand herself until an early frost that third October put down a black ice unexpected in the night, and she drove to early Mass and hit the brakes fast on a curve at the shake of something in her peripheral vision. Her rear wheels froze. She spun out and off the road and raced down the Kittree's handsome hill to the decorative pond and sank. Passenger side aimed like an arrow to the muck that held the lilies tight at the bottom. She watched the water rise as calmly as she might watch a faucet filling a pitcher. She knew she'd want to go home now, once she stepped out of the car, she'd have to miss Mass this one morning. The water was at her knees when she detached her house key from the ring, when she pushed open with a force she didn't know she had, the water already pushing back against her door, and slugged out and waded, making havoc with Margaret Kittree's dormant flowers, making a mess, she told Kathleen. How will I ever apologize? That kind of thing takes years to develop and there I am, a lunatic out of nowhere. God forgive me. Everyone forgave her, and suggested Valium, Wellbutrin, Prozac, a grief group. But who could she possibly sit with who might look her in the eye and smile and say I know you. Besides, she had no time for groups, never had.

But then she'd had the idea, and maybe, if she was honest, it came from Kathleen and her endless chatter about doing good for the children in Africa. This was the substitute for romance with the Henderson boy. Or maybe no substitute, what could she really know these days. But why Africa, she thought, why not just here? There was one family in Rumson who'd lost a father. Ann McCleary invited the widow to tea. She used all her kindness, and spoke as she would, as she already had, to any one of her own children. When she left the pretty girl with the dark bob—whose eyes, Ann hoped, would be less dark in time—when she backed away down the drive Ann gave a sweet wave and called good-bye. Good-bye.

But what about Holy Cross. She knew everything there was to know about children and many times she'd served as chaperone, as helper. For someone as agile and as knowledgeable as herself, some use could surely be found.

A library? she said to Sister Mary Arthur. Ann had no wish to disguise her detachment, detachment was her best friend. Are you thinking of building something, then? Maybe take over Father's precious garage.

No, no, not a bit, Ann, no, not in the least. I thought of something roving. Something that floats a bit, she laughed, and Ann always appreciated that laugh, and wondered how in these years it hadn't lost its light touch. Ann was listening, waiting to hear the laugh again: that's how she does it. I know all your tricks, Sister, she said.

It will be a bit of a trick and I need a conjurer, will you help me?

It was a graceless thing, her cart. The wheels squeaked and the wire mesh caught at the pages and grilled them, engraved them with a crisscross. But this was the library Sister had in mind. Ann McCleary could choose her beneficiaries at will, one kindergarten, two first grades, two second grades. Why not Tuesdays, Sister said, Tuesday mornings, nine to noon. Mrs. Guski will keep us in literature, and keep the cart locked safely in the supply closet. And here was her first battle. Mrs. Guski thought literature for small first readers involved saints and martyrs. Lurid paintings, the wounds especially crimson; even in her day the illustrations weren't so gruesome. No, she wouldn't read them, wouldn't even carry them. Ann McCleary held her ground and had soon tucked in books of her own, things she'd found on bookshelves kept for the towheads. And she wandered when she didn't mean to, just popping into the A&P for some radishes but she'd find herself next-door in Sally Hetzler's bookstore, who gave her a discount for the library, and she became a regular customer.

The children weren't much interested. They had grandmothers of their own, and even Holy Cross had computers in the kindergarten. She never spoke about this to Mary Arthur, never said she wasn't quite as welcome as she'd hoped. And once, when the blank faces greeted her as a stranger, even the teacher couldn't make her out, she'd wheeled her awkward cart all the way out to Father's garage and wept beside the Karmann Ghia where no one would think to look for her. She was not a quitter. But now she wondered why that mattered, that quality. She'd already held a high head, but maybe life shifted. Maybe the things that sustained you just wore out and new things, new people, needed other qualities, and yours just went to sleep. Sometimes a life just finished, unexpectedly, and it was the ones still wandering around in foolish stiff bodies after they were already done who were the sorry ones. She cried and cried and no one came to comfort her because who could.

Ann McCleary told her children when they were small, when things were hard, if they were sick, or especially for the older ones, for Terry, when their father died and they were too little to lose him, she told them that one day they would realize they were better, and that they'd been better for a while. They hadn't noticed the shift, it came so quietly, and that was God's grace, she believed it, and she told them it was true. Only Terry gave her a hard time. He dove off the high dive two summers after his father's death, and by a wicked chance made the inward arc just to the spot where his chin cracked the tile edge. Blood bloomed out into the deep end and she caught him first, unconscious, the concussion a sure thing, and forty stitches in two layers, and black eyes, both, and bruises on the shoulders, a mess, a terrible mess, and she was forced to revise her theory, her theology. Sometimes the pain needs to reverberate for a long time, for longer than even you or anyone else might think necessary or fair. Sometimes that's how it goes, and God may or may not be a part of that, probably is, she told her boy. But it's anyone's guess, she said, surprising herself in the admittance. And later she remembered a smile in him, a long time later, too long she thought, when the others had bounced back, to her credit everyone said, they admired her, everyone did, to her credit her children thrived. And one day, Terry smiled a smile she recognized in her deepest self. He pulled a bit of onion grass out by the root; she just happened to spot him through her kitchen window. He was almost nine, now, and not so tall, with beautiful hands, like his father's, long, someone made for a piano. Up came the grass, roots and blades and he examined it all closely, the whole package clutched in his hand and he smiled at the shape and the sharp stink of the roots. He put his face close, then wrenched back and laughed, his face so happy, and then happy to be happy, the double-happiness smile she called it, so hard won, and it never left him after that, it became the way he smiled, the way he lit every room he ever walked into.

There were Tuesdays and more Tuesdays and they got used to her, and didn't stare when she pushed her squeaky cart into the classroom and took her time lowering herself into the armchair Sister Mary Arthur had placed in each classroom to accommodate her floating library. More like a falling library, they said, our reader falls asleep! And so she did every once in a while on those warm spring mornings. When the five-year-olds lay out their mats and curled on the floor like kittens, she dozed, too, the sound of her own voice putting her to sleep, sometimes first of all. She knew they complained about her. What part of a progressive curriculum did she serve? But Sister Mary Arthur was adamant, and Mrs. Guski whispered it was one of her *conceptions*. It's a charity case, said Mrs. Kelly, who taught the brighter first grade. It's fortunate I didn't quite hear that, Mrs. Kelly. Sister Mary Arthur's door was open, and even Mrs. Guski froze. But nothing more was said about it after that. And Ann McCleary became part of the landscape, along with the candy sales and the beanies worn to Mass.

There was a little boy, of course, after a year or two, in the kindergarten, who didn't entirely dislike a story read out loud. His parents were nostalgic that way, and she let him chew on

the covers of the books she wasn't reading. Still teething are we?
A big boy like you? And he smiled at her, and then a sly film of
a second smile came, too, he had to pull the thick cardboard cover
away to accommodate his own full delight. Look at you, she
laughed, a double happiness. He dropped the book and tumbled
off. His attention snapped away in an instant. But a few weeks
later it happened again, though now she knew to watch and
wait was death. She'd only catch it by the very quietest chance,
she told Kathleen. And only now and then.

Acknowledgments

I wish to acknowledge the beautiful work of: Melanie Jackson, Elisabeth Schmitz, Jessica Monahan, Brigid Hughes, Fiona Maazel, Elizabeth Gaffney, Anne McPeak, Stanley Lindberg, Don Lee, David Daniel, Madison Smartt Bell, Beth Bosworth, Meredith Broussard, Rick Moody, Jennifer Egan, Ruth Danon, always Gary Giddins; everyone in Liam Rector's extraordinary community at Bennington, especially Susan Cheever, Amy Hempel, Sheila Kohler, Charles Bock, Bob Shacochis, Mohammed Naseehu Ali, Priscilla Hodgkins, David Gates, and every dance with Jason Shinder; in the Hudson Valley, Louis Asekoff, Martin Epstein, Romulus Linney, Carole Maso, and Mary Gaitskill. Thanks to the Corporation of Yaddo and to the MacDowell Colony. Thanks to my family, always the McCarthys, Shaheens, and Hetzlers. I hold my mother and father and brother close in memory with love. I thank Duke Beeson, heart and soul, for his abiding, astonishing generosity.

DOUBLE HAPPINESS

MARY-BETH HUGHES

ABOUT THIS GUIDE

We hope that these discussion questions
will enhance your reading group's exploration
of Mary-Beth Hughes's *Double Happiness*. They are
meant to stimulate discussion, offer new viewpoints,
and enrich your enjoyment of the book.

More reading group guides and additional information,
including summaries, author tours, and author sites for
other fine Black Cat titles, may be found on
our Web site, www.groveatlantic.com.

QUESTIONS FOR DISCUSSION

1. These stories have a surface lucidity that goes down briskly. But often time bombs have been set that detonate as one reads on. Rereading reveals even more buried explosives. Which stories operated this way for you? Go back and trace some of the clues that may have eluded you at first.

2. What is meant by the title "Pelican Song"? How close to the mark was old Sven growling over the speakerphone at Christmas (p. 13)? How could the title also relate, at least ironically, to the legend of pelican mothers pecking out their own blood to feed their starving chicks?

3. "Pelican Song" contains a recurring concern for women in these stories: body image. "My biggest obstacle to respect, however, had to do with men. I had an odd figure for a modern dancer. Rubenesque, my composer boyfriend called my body when pressed for compliments. . . . I believed a body could be different and still be okay. But when the composer mentioned Botero, I lost confidence" (p. 3). It's a funny picture for us, those balloon-like sculptures marching up Park Avenue, but what can it mean for a dancer? How does her weight reflect or cause other problems in her life? What other stories in the book come to mind here? In "Aces" Raymond attacks Megan soon after

the wedding, when she has been less watchful than before. "You look like a fat little boy," he says, and she'd been on a diet ever since (p. 131). How else does size figure in the story? Helena? Megan's "joyful" pregnancy a decade later?

4. Hughes sets the mood in "Horse" with a cold, drab, gray seaside honeymoon and an insensitive, self-absorbed husband. How does the bride, Isabel, struggle to connect? What is symbolized by the beautiful white horse in captivity? How does Isabel break Tom's shell of cold indifference?

5. Eden in "Blue Grass" says "I hate this about myself, crying all the time, and I know without a mirror that mascara has made two black half-moons under my eyes, which look ghoulish. . . . When I stand up from the white iron deck chair, the whole back of my dress is wet with dew. I pull the fabric away from my legs" (pp. 44–45). Hughes is unafraid to depict awkward, self-conscious women who may not be beautiful, but are painfully real. How has the beautiful sister Cara affected Eden? Talk about her "pilgrimage" to Saks Fifth Avenue seeking "some device or potion, some answer" from Rita, the "conjurer" saleswoman (p. 27). Which other women in the stories try to change themselves to accommodate a man or standard of beauty like the "sliver-hipped blonde" Eden imagines on the Vineyard (p. 36)?

6. "Mixed marriage. That's the trouble. Nothing could be plainer," say the Benjamis in "Roundup" (p. 53). What does the title refer to? How does it date the story? What does the term imply about our democratic process? On the other side of the family, how does Lucy Twitchell's May-flower family react to her marriage? What would it be like to be married to Philip? Is he ever unambiguously accepting of anyone? His wife ("Miss Two Left Hands" p. 63), his daughter, even his dog, Gunner? How does the issue of suing snake through the story? Beyond mixed marriage, what are the fears of contagion and infection?

7. Talk about the vulnerable but plucky child in the story "Rome," trying to make sense of the world and her father. "On the street it was snowing harder now. The daylight was gray and dim but the Plaza lights were bright. The doorman's booth glittered like a fortune-teller's at a carnival. She knew her father was waiting for her, but Olivia felt a strong undertow of hesitation" (p. 81). How does this passage capture both the glitter and the menace of the story? Look at these details on page 74–75: "On Saturday?" "She reached for the soup pot, forgetting the mitt." "Her mother's sudden kiss felt dry and too light, like a dead bug blown across her cheek." "[Her mother] looked to Olivia like a big wishbone strained to the limit." All these moments happen as the distracted parents send a third-grader

on the train into the city alone. "She'd never been allowed to go anywhere in New York alone before. Her father must be making a mistake that he would realize in a moment" (p. 80). What are the successive sinking insights Olivia gleans about her father? Is the town chauffeur, Nat, the only person who is truly careful about Olivia?

8. In "Israel" how are the ideas of death, rebirth, neglect, abuse, and forgiveness knit together? "Dr. Ovita was talking about physical therapy, not magic. There was nothing magical about Dr. Ovita, which is why I liked him. He never disappeared; he never changed shape" (p. 92). What are the consequences of the father's hovering between two worlds in the nine months since he deserted the family? What are the results of the daughter's moving to Israel? Do you see a parallel with the end of "Pelican Song"?

9. "The Widow of Combarelles," the longest story, is a tantalizing whorl that coils and spirals with events, memories, and innuendoes. What do you make of Patty? A silver stiletto in a garden glove, how does she reveal herself to the reader through her own deliciously self-deluding strategies? Her story is part Austen's *Emma*, part Charles Addams, with some Blanche of *Streetcar Named Desire* and Amanda of *The Glass Menagerie*. Talk about her artfulness. Are characters left wounded in her wake? "She

told him it was funny, his father had made his first million when he was even younger than Brad was now. Amazing, right?" (p. 108). What are the exceptions? Who stands up to her and how? Show how the tale is told through Patty, who persists in thinking she is a loyal friend ("Aid and comfort, aid and comfort" p. 103); a graceful, generous, if unappreciated, hostess; and irresistible, well-preserved belle. Rarely, Patty slips her manners: "Where the hell were her slippers anyway?" (p. 109) and "Lifeless rot, both of them" (p. 116). Rot and decay she usually ignores or dismisses. Give examples. How does the book title *Double Happiness* give a clue to Patty's mentality? Behind the merry widow tale lies the original "Widow of Combarelles" and echoes of the war in France. How do the double stories intersect? How does Guy serve as a moral compass even as Patty sets her sights? "But for now she knew to keep still. Let him sip and think as if she were nothing but a vapor, or maybe she would be a flame. His choice" (p. 126).

10. Adultery may split marriages, be ignored or forestalled in four of the stories placed in the middle of *Double Happiness*. In "Aces," there is a theatrical nexus of old girlfriend, husband, and wife meeting by chance in a café in Rome. The husband, Ray, responds to the girlfriend with "'You remember Megan, of course.' And Megan stood, too, belly

pushed forward. She offered her hand and the victor's smile he'd seen before" (p. 131). Does Raymond enjoy the frisson of the moment, even as he recalls he'd been "a bit of a bastard" (p. 132)? How? To whom? He's a man who wants things calm, his way, who looks appreciatively at a veiled woman in a newsreel because she keeps so much inside. Is he a case study in infidelity? "All the tears, all the drama. Not some fateful twine of love and work, as Helena had claimed. Just *hormones*, Megan's favorite word" (p. 132). What role does Kamal play in the story? What is his fate? Trace the pattern of Raymond's treachery in "Aces." What does that title mean? Is Raymond, the future father, really free of Helena?

11. In "May Day," how would you describe the aging parents waiting at the Rhinecliff train station for Melody, their long-grown daughter? What is the occasion? What is the weather on the Hudson? Why is the husband forlorn? May flowers are delinquent: "wisteria hung with desiccated fronds. 'Wouldn't you know it,' said his wife" (p. 152). John Updike wrote, "Old age, he was discovering, arrived in increments of uncertainty" (a story called "Free"). Can this be the mother gripping the railing, stepping carefully as she descends to the platform? Melody, once off the train, responds to her mother with "Hey, Daphne, hi. . . . And quick as a leaf brush, the dry tired peck" of a kiss (p. 175).

The mother wonders at how silly it is that this "this teetering frowning wretch" who won't even call her Mother can make her so happy (p. 154). The father in turn, excited, says "Boat's in the water." "'You think I'd miss it,' asked the girl, who looked committed to missing everything" (p. 155). What creates the cruel insouciance of grown children, like this "child" of thirty-five with the misnomer of Melody who comes home after years to feel "quick and light and lovely" while her father struggles up a long staircase with her suitcase?

12. Does the title "Guidance" seem to relate to Fawn's life from Denmark to Tokyo to Djakarta to Kuala Lumpur? Why does Betsy say "Just call him Mommy" about the old American? (p. 165). What happens to jostle Fawn's absorption with her legs, naked swims, and pregnancy? "Up until my birthday at the Hilton I never really took guns seriously" (p. 163). How are Americans depicted? Her husband? Officials in Kuala Lumpur? What is the role of Mustache? How much do we trust the instincts of this teenage narrator with her "fluid, unpredictable style of friendship" (p. 182)? "Betsy always said I had a fatality imagination. Not that I foresaw the worst, the opposite: I saw love and opportunity in every future, and that was fatal" (p. 175). What can become of Fawn and her twins?

13. What is the irony of the title "Double Happiness" for the last story? There are, after all, two devastating deaths in Ann McCleary's life in a New Jersey still in the lost shadow of the fallen towers. Is it surprising that Ann returns to the school that has helped her raise five children when she looks for a job? What is the most vivid memory for her in the waiting room? What has propelled her here at this time? What are the series of afflictions that culminate in the Kitrees' pond? What is symbolized by the young Terry's pulling up onion grass (see p. 197) and how is that moment inevitably connected with the little boy at the end "who didn't entirely dislike a story read out loud" (p. 198). Is Ann McCleary both hopeful and realistic in choosing life over her "proclivity to slip away" (p. 193)? Why is this story not only the title story of the book but chosen to be at the end? Is it a kind of summing up? A valedictory?